THE HEART'S HOME

BY
JUDITH ANSELL

MILLS & BOON LIMITED
ETON HOUSE   18-24 PARADISE ROAD
RICHMOND   SURREY   TW9 1SR

D0227447

CHAPTER ONE

BENEATH the aircraft's wings, the plains of the Sudan spread out endlessly, from this height a uniform reddish-brown, meeting a clear blue sky at the ends of the earth. It was hot in the plane. Gena was glad she'd chosen white to wear. It was the coolest colour, though the straight denim skirt did not allow much circulation of air. She had taken the jacket off long ago, and rolled the short sleeves of her shirt up even higher on to her arms.

The pilot appreciated her choice of dress too. It set off her shapely form to perfection, and contrasted nicely with the golden tone of her skin. He turned to look for a moment and grinned to himself. What would they make of this little thing in Udari? he wondered. Well, it was almost time to find out. Time to start their descent.

On the rough landing-ground at Udari, two kilometres from the hospital and the centre of the Sudan Medical Service in this part of the country, Richard Maddison stood waiting for his new assistant. He hoped the Health Authority had chosen well this time. It was too disruptive, having doctors come and go. The people needed to get to know them.

This woman looked good on paper. Too young, certainly, but there were good reports of her work,

5

and she'd worked as a student with the Aboriginal people in Australia. Coming from Australia was in itself a plus; she'd be used to the heat more than Britons. There were still days when Richard hated it himself.

He straightened his tall body and raised a brown, good-looking face to the sun, and in doing so caught sight of the silver speck in the blue, the plane from Khartoum.

'There it is,' said Angus Cameron. The older man, his friend and deputy, had also caught sight of the bright insect descending towards their desolate little strip. Angus wiped his round red face with a linen handkerchief. 'Hope this lady doctor likes the heat, eh, Richard?' he said in his bluff, good-humoured manner.

'Mm,' said Richard. 'And flies and hyenas and sandstorms and warring tribespeople too.'

Angus laughed. 'Ha, ha! Yes, we'd better hope she's tough, hadn't we?'

The Udari Central Hospital had never had a female doctor before. It had European nurses, of course, whose job it was to provide the skills that the local nurses lacked, and to train the locals towards self-sufficiency. There were three now— Matron Potts and Sisters Hickey and Anderson. They were tough, self-reliant women who worked hard, made difficult decisions, often on their own, and who could turn their hands to almost anything if they had to, in the absence of men.

At the end of the makeshift runway, the plane

seemed to hover, melting in the heat haze, then dropped towards the red earth, kissed it with its wheels once, twice, and finally bumped down, bucketing along the ground with clouds of red dust flying. It came to a halt, and the dust began to settle, only to be churned up again by the two Africans who wheeled a low set of steps to its side.

Doctors Maddison and Cameron waited, brushing the flies away. The aircraft door folded back. The pilot appeared and handed two bags to the waiting natives. He descended the steps and turned to the young woman alighting from the plane into the arid heat of the Central African desert.

She paused for a moment on the top step and looked out into the empty landscape, a petite figure in form-fitting white, golden hair in waves gleaming in the African sun. The corners of a charming mouth lifted, and she smiled. She was beautiful.

Richard Maddison, standing stock-still by the truck, groaned aloud. 'Oh, my God!' he said. 'What the hell have they sent us?'

Angus Cameron whistled softly.

Gena's pulse-rate was abnormally high as the plane touched down and bumped along the runway. She knew she ought to be tired after the long haul from Sydney to Nairobi, a few hours' sleep, then on to Khartoum and Udari, but adrenalin buoyed her up.

She could see a shed at the end of the runway, and, drawn up beside it, a Land Rover and some people. What would they be like, she wondered,

these people she was destined to spend the next year
with? She hoped they would be easy to get along
with, and reflected that she'd never had any trouble
getting on with people before. She had always
possessed a pretty sure instinct for what other people
were feeling, and, coupled with a natural tact, it had
made her a very satisfactory colleague.

Despite these comforting reflections, Gena found
her heart was trotting along at an even greater rate
when she climbed down from the aircraft and walked
towards two European men, one short and fat with
a shiny face, one tall and lean, his face half hidden
by his hat. The short fat man was striding towards
her and arrived before his companion. He threw out
his hand.

'Angus Cameron, my dear. You must be Dr
Lamb.'

She gripped his hand firmly and smiled at the
obvious friendliness of his welcome. 'Gena,' she
said.

The tall man reached them, and Gena turned. She
raised her eyes to his face, and an instant shock ran
through her. He was uncommonly good-looking.
Gena felt herself begin to blush at the thought, and
hastily held out her hand and stammered her name.

He paused a moment before he took it, then
pressed it for the briefest instant. 'Richard Maddison,'
he said in a deep, well-educated voice, then the lips
that had uttered it folded back into the grimmest
line she had ever seen, below eyes of flint.

Angus Cameron made a nervous movement.

'Er—this way to the car, my dear. We'll get out of this rotten heat.'

As they walked towards the Land Rover, all Gena's instincts told her that Richard Maddison was one man who was anything but glad to make her acquaintance. In the truck, on the short drive out to the hospital, he gripped the steering-wheel with strong brown hands and was utterly silent.

Angus Cameron chatted to the girl. She sat in the back with him, being jolted delightfully against him over the almost non-existent road. What a surprise the girl was! 'What made you want to come out here, my dear?' he asked, and saw Richard Maddison glance backwards in the mirror as though he too was silently asking that question.

Gena turned deep blue eyes to Dr Cameron and considered this kind-looking, fat Englishman, so out of place in this spot himself. She smiled. 'There were so many reasons,' she said quietly. 'Perhaps the most important one is that life has always been so easy for me. I've had so much of everything.'

The sound from the front seat might have been a stifled groan. But Angus Cameron, faced with those clear blue eyes, rather understood.

CHAPTER TWO

THE hospital buildings stood together on a gentle rise in the ground. They were single-storeyed and rectangular, and both ward block and residence had a wide veranda almost all around. At the eastern end of the ward block was a low addition whose sign announced 'Clinic'. There were rough wooden benches outside it, crowded into the shade of a straggly tree.

Beyond the wards, on the opposite side to the residence, was a haphazard collection of buildings in cement and corrugated iron. They were the services buildings—workshops, kitchen, laundry. And further away, standing alone, there was a structure which, by the constant drone which came from it, declared itself to be the generating plant.

The ward block and residence were not unattractive, thought Gena, with their long, low, whitewashed walls and wide verandas.

In a little time they were sitting on the veranda of the residence in a collection of rickety wicker chairs, with the sun sinking into the western plains. It was cooler now, and the landscape, with the redness of the soil accentuated by the dying sun, quite beautiful. Gena, standing at the veranda rail, cool drink in hand, said so.

Richard Maddison glanced at her briefly, his face still set in uncompromising grimness. 'I'm afraid you'll find enough ugliness out here to outweigh the effect of one sunset, Dr Lamb.' His tone was faintly scornful.

She studied the doctor, who had looked away again. Not terribly old, she thought—thirties. Powerful, with broad shoulders and strong thighs. And, as she had observed before, very good-looking. She wondered what had brought him here, and could not help thinking of Peter for a moment. Richard Maddison was both physician and surgeon, and could have commanded a very comfortable life in London. Half the nurses he met would fall in love with him, Gena thought.

'There is beauty too, though, Richard,' said Angus, and raised himself from his chair. He walked to the veranda's edge and faced the south-east. 'Look in that direction, Dr Lamb.'

Gena corrected him gently. 'Please, Dr Cameron —Gena.'

'Angus, my dear,' he said kindly. 'Look.'

Gena gazed out over the patchy dry grass in front of the hospital with its scattered stunted trees, over the huddled huts of the town, lying in a small depression half a mile distant.

'Those are the Nuba Mountains you see.'

They rose beyond the plain, a collection of rounded hills, roseate in this light but spread with a soft dark green in the folds of their valleys where the vegetation grew best.

'Mm.' Gena made a small sound of appreciation.

'The Nuba people, the people of those mountains, were once a great tribe who inhabited most of western and central Sudan,' he said. 'With the Arab invaders, they shrank back, you see, and sought the shelter of those hills.' Angus sipped at his drink. 'They were a collection of tribes, really,' he continued. 'The Africans in this area belong mostly to one of the Nuba tribes, the Atema. They are a very admirable people, intelligent, resourceful, warm-hearted—very proud. They still retain the old hostility towards the Arab, which makes life hard at times. The Arabs of this region aren't bad chaps, mind you. They're camel herders still. It's surprising really how much of traditional life is retained by both Arab and African here, only four hundred kilometres from Khartoum.'

Only four hundred kilometres, thought Gena. They had the same sense of distance here as they did in the Australian outback, she reflected. There, people often drove a hundred and fifty kilometres to go to the pictures—the cinema, these people would call it. But, as it was in outback Australia, that four hundred kilometres could take a long, long time to cover if conditions were bad and things went wrong.

Matron Elinor Potts spoke for the first time since their introduction. 'It's the Arabs from further away that cause the trouble. They have a stranglehold on commerce, and it's their tradition to cheat, I'm afraid. They exploit the Africans and even their own less sophisticated brothers. Sometimes World Food

Programme items turn up on the Arab trading trucks. They sell them to the people who were meant to get them for free.'

Gena, frowning at this, noticed Richard Maddison's eyes upon her. His mouth had a sardonic twist. 'You will find human nature displayed for you out here in all its glory,' he said.

'Ah!' An exclamation came from Angus, inclining his ear to the east. 'That'll be Jonathan.' And Gena could hear it now—the low thrum of a Land Rover engine, with soon the changing note as it pulled up the rise in front of the hospital. It rolled to a halt in the yard between the wards and residence, and a surprising number of Africans piled out of its cabin and dropped off the burdened luggage racks on its roof.

Presently a slim young man detached himself from behind the wheel and moved with the grace of a cat to the veranda steps which he sprang up with a readiness that belied the day's heat. 'Where's our new colleague?' he cried. 'I've driven all the way from Kepa through sandstorms and hostile natives to welcome her!'

Gena laughed and got to her feet, ready to shake hands with Dr Jonathan Haywood, the last of the medical staff of Udari.

He did not advance to meet her, however, but appeared to stand transfixed, one lock of straight blond hair hanging over light blue eyes that mirrored his surprise.

'Gena Lamb,' she said to smooth the introduction.

'Can't be,' the young man said emphatically, shaking his blond head. 'I know for a fact you're not a doctor.'

Richard Maddison shifted in his chair and looked as though he might speak, but Jonathan continued before he could do so.

'My dear girl, all female doctors are overweight and frumpy, wear hornrimmed spectacles and have abundant hair on their upper lips.' He paused. 'You don't have hair on your upper lip at all,' he said accusingly.

Gena rocked with laughter. 'Well,' she said at length, 'you'll just have to take it on faith, then. I am a doctor,' then added as an afterthought, 'though a very junior one, I must admit. I'm hoping you'll all be kind enough to give me advice and teach me things.'

'My dear, of course,' murmured Angus. 'Anything at all. At any time.' He smiled at her.

Jonathan Haywood gave him a look of amused tolerance. Silly old goat, he might have been thinking. He's in love with her already.

His gaze also took in Richard Maddison, who was looking decidedly not in love, and in fact not even amused. He looked up at Jonathan. 'How was Kepa?' he asked.

'Busy,' said Jonathan, wrinkling his brow. 'A lot of diarrhoea, of course, but also some measles.'

'Oh, dear!' said Matron Potts. Measles, such a benign childhood illness at home, could sweep through the countryside here, decimating the infant population like King Herod's campaign.

'You didn't need to bring any in to the hospital?' Matron asked.

'None that bad as yet,' he replied. 'But we can expect it. I'll have to go back—I only really came back here because I was low on water.'

He turned innocent eyes to Richard Maddison, who looked as though he didn't believe it, but forbore to accuse his young assistant of wasting an enormous amount of expensive fuel in order to have a look at the new doctor.

'I might go myself,' said Richard.

It was the function of this hospital to act as the headquarters for the Medical Service in this part of the Sudan. From the hospital, health patrols went out for days or weeks at a time, camping along the way and bringing something of modern medicine to the people who couldn't come to the hospital. Sometimes people were brought back by the patrol for a stay in the ward. The health problems of the Sudan were immense, as in all the African countries. One in four children made it to one year of age and the average life expectancy was forty-six for men, and forty-nine for women. With leprosy, sleeping sickness and bilharzia, things would have been grim even without a food and water problem. But the drought and the ever-increasing encroachment of the desert had made starvation and the diseases which go along with it the major problem.

Jonathan helped himself to a drink, and settled in

a chair next to Gena. Presently a pretty red-haired girl appeared to join them, and was introduced as Sister Heather Anderson. She was cheerful and talkative, and fired a barrage of questions at Gena in a friendly way, hardly waiting for answers, but chattering on about Gena and Udari and herself. Gena wondered where she got the energy at the end of a stifling day, and doubted whether she herself had that sort of stamina. Too much of Heather alone would wear her out!

Sitting back in the twilight, Gena began to play a game that she and her father used to play. If this person were an animal, what sort would they be?

Matron Potts was a draught horse, she thought, large and lumbering and kind, a little slow perhaps and a bit ungainly, but immensely strong and reliable. Just the sort of person to run a hospital out here. Nothing would overwhelm her. She would always be calm and caring.

Heather was a squirrel, a quick, industrious, energetic animal who was seldom still. Even now she was kicking the leg of her chair and squirming restlessly.

Angus was a big friendly dog, an intelligent one like a St Bernard.

And Jonathan? She had almost chosen a gazelle, but no, that seemed a little timid for him. Some sort of cat, she thought, graceful, but perhaps with hidden claws.

That left Richard. She was studying him speculatively with her head on one side, when he turned to catch her at it. He raised one eyebrow very slightly in something that looked like derision. And as Gena flushed to the roots of her hair, she suddenly knew what he was. He was a bull— powerful, male and dangerous.

'Where's Sister Hickey?' Angus asked Matron. 'She's the last of our European staff,' he explained to Gena.

'Probably praying,' said Jonathan in an under-tone, but not softly enough to escape a frown from Matron.

'I'll go and find her,' said that worthy woman. 'She was worried about one of the children, but she must meet Dr Lamb.'

This last introduction was soon effected, with Matron Potts returning in the company of a tall dark girl, plain but with unusual eyes. They were large and dark, almost black, and burnt with a peculiar feverish intensity that had earned Pauline Hickey the fear of some of the natives.

'How is your patient?' asked Angus kindly.

Pauline shook her head slowly, her dark eyes large and tragic. 'I've been praying for her,' she said tonelessly.

Jonathan gave Gena a gentle nudge.

That night, under the mosquito netting in her room in the quiet house, Gena found she could not sleep. Instead she relived the scenes, one fond, one pain-ful, that had taken place twelve thousand miles away on the eve of her departure.

'If you go to Udari, I won't be here when you get

back,' Peter had said, and with a fresh stab of pain she saw his face again, the pleasant features marred by anger and chagrin. In the dark she felt for the place where the engagement ring had been, and was no more. And then, as though to comfort her, the image of her parents rose instead.

'It may be for the best,' the elder Dr Lamb, her father, had said. 'Your mother and I are fond of Peter, but he doesn't have your strength, or the same values.'

He hadn't understood her—that was certain. Life had been so good to Gena, and all over the world were children born to starve, to die violently or from diseases that should be readily cured. How could he fail to share her need to give something back?

Gena sighed. And it was borne in upon her with oppressive weight as she lay in the utter stillness of the desert, with only the hum of the hospital generator in the distance, how alone she was now.

Perhaps in time these people would be her friends, but for the present they were strangers. And her life could be in their hands soon. Who knew what they might encounter in the miles of empty desert on patrols? Gena shivered. It was true what they said—the desert could be cold at night. Australia was different. There, hot days were followed by sultry nights, and tossing and turning to find a cooler spot under the fan.

Suddenly she longed for the coastal town that was her home—for the security of her parents, the green tree-filled garden where the cicadas sang in summer, the blue rollers of the Pacific and the distant euca-lypt-covered mountains.

She thought again about her colleagues. Jonathan Haywood—slim and elegant, with an irreverent sense of humour and undeniable charm. He would be fun, she thought, and perhaps a friend. Matron Potts—deep-bosomed, warm-hearted, wise, some-one to rely on for help and advice. Good-humoured Angus, already accepting her as one of them. Heather, not too much older than she, and sure to be cheerful company. Pauline—a horse of a differ-ent colour. A strange-looking woman, but she'd got on with stranger before.

Almost unwillingly her mind turned to Dr Maddison, the boss, and she wondered whether he wasn't the source of much of her unease—grim, taciturn, disapproving. Gena frowned to herself. Why should that be so? He didn't even know her. He couldn't dislike her on sight, could he? She couldn't recall that anyone had done so before.

And yet she had not imagined it, the displeasure on his face at the airstrip, and the disapproval since. The only faintly comforting thought Gena had was that maybe he was like that with all newcomers. She would just have to win him round.

But even this positive thought didn't bring the sleep that she needed so badly. Finally she sat up on the side of the bed and fought her way free of the mosquito netting. Quietly she slipped to the window and looked out, and at once caught her breath at the splendid vision of the desert sky—deepest purple, with more stars than she had seen in her life before.

Gena stayed for a while looking at the night sky of Africa and, when at last she lay down again, it was with a new calm and a sense that everything would be all right. After all, she thought sleepily, she was here to do a job for people who needed her. That was her main concern. She determined to do it well.

CHAPTER THREE

JONATHAN watched the three figures walk across from the wards in the midday sun, and smiled at the incongruity of the small neat figure in khaki drill shorts and shirt between the two large figures of the men. She was certainly a turn-up for the books, he thought. What could a girl who looked like that want in a place like this? And wasn't Maddison seriously displeased about it?

He had listened quietly last night while Angus and Richard had discussed it after Gena had gone to bed.

'It's beyond me how they could have chosen someone so unsuitable to be sent out here!' Maddison had stormed.

'Oh, my dear chap, I don't know. . .' said Angus.

Maddison gave a snort of impatience. 'Use your head, Angus!' he snapped. 'What am I going to do with a piece of Dresden china on a patrol when I'm bogged in the sand up to my axles? Can you see her helping to dig us out? If she gets out in the sun, she'll shrivel up, with that colouring!'

Jonathan smiled to himself in the dark at the description. It was very apt. She was like one of those china dolls, in colouring and form, at least. But she wasn't stiff. She was graceful, in fact.

'Mmm. . .' Angus rubbed his nose uncomfortably. 'Not any fairer than Heather, though,' he observed justly. 'And she looks as if she tans.'

But it wasn't Maddison's only objection. 'She's far too young. Young for her age, in fact—she looks like a child. Do you think she'll carry the authority to influence the native people, to persuade them to take our medicines and change their way of doing things?' He didn't wait for an answer. 'Is she likely to be able to work for days in the searing heat with little sleep when there's an epidemic?' He lapsed into disgusted silence.

Angus watched his old friend for a while. He had known Richard Maddison from boyhood, had encouraged him, in fact, to follow his inclination and become a doctor. He knew the dedication of the man, the depth of feeling he had for these African people and their troubles. Angus had been one of the few not to register surprise when it was known that Richard Maddison intended not to take the important post at St Thomas's Hospital, but rather to disappear to some God-forsaken region of central Africa. But then few people came to know Richard Maddison well. The surprising thing was that it was his patients who felt they knew the man the best. His caring and compassion were transparently honest.

Angus decided to take the bull by the horns. 'My dear boy,' he said gruffly, using the address he had always unconsciously adopted when endeavouring to instruct his rather headstrong young friend in earlier days, 'don't be too hasty. I don't say you're not right, of course. It may have been a mistake. But at this point, don't you see, there's no evidence on the matter.' He cleared his throat and touched the younger man on the shoulder. 'What I'm saying, Richard, is don't condemn the girl. Give her a chance.'

Now the three came up the steps into the grateful shade of the veranda. They had spent the morning showing Gena the hospital, demonstrating the often primitive ways that things had to be done there and introducing her to the patients and the native nursing staff. It was a far cry from the Royal William in Sydney where Gena had trained.

The African servant, Gudwe, appeared in the doorway. 'Lunch,' he said, indicating the dining-room with an inclination of his head.

It was at once too much and too little to call this man a servant. He was equally at home pulling the carburettor of one of the trucks to pieces as serving their luncheon. And this was not the British Raj. This was Africa, and Gudwe was an Atema and as good as any white man—better than most, in fact, for white men, for all their superior technology, did incomprehensible things. He, Gudwe, had seen them, and laughed till his stomach hurt.

He looked at the white girl again now. He had first met her at breakfast, and wanted to reach out and touch her to make sure she was real. White people felt this was rude, however, so he didn't. He just contented himself with grinning and shaking his head and making the peculiar 'Ee-ee' sound of his tribe when they could not believe their eyes.

It was much the same sort of response that Jonathan still encountered when remote villagers caught sight of his shock of blond hair. After all, it was not the colour for hair. Hair for humans was dark. And here was this human, the colour of a young goat.

Gudwe knew what he would do if he were this girl's father: he would marry her with Jonathan. What fine babies they would have! They were a matching pair.

As they sat down to their midday meal, Gudwe made sure that Gena was next to Jonathan. The dining-room was a spacious apartment that gave on to the veranda. A long refectory table dominated the room and a rather ill-matching set of chairs was ranged around it. Above them a fan turned, and moved the hot air a little; otherwise the room was empty except for a battered sideboard, on which Gudwe now dumped dishes unceremoniously. They helped themselves from the sideboard, Jonathan kindly contributing a commentary on the food.

'And this is sweet potato,' he said. 'You'll like that at first, and then in a few weeks you'll have had so much of it that you'll never want to see it again!'

Actually, Gena had always liked sweet potato, which was eaten a lot at home. Some of the other things were rather more peculiar, she thought, but no doubt she'd get used to them too. What she did need to do, she decided, was find a cushion for her chair. Since Gudwe had chosen her chair with her matrimonial prospects in mind rather than her comfort, and it had turned out to be not the highest one available, the large refectory table came halfway up her chest. It made it awkward to eat.

She asked whether there might be a cushion around, and Matron Potts assured her that they would find one, and swap her chair as well.

'Perhaps we should have a high-chair made for you, Dr Lamb,' said Richard Maddison in a tone of dry humour.

Gena looked up at him. She would have accepted it as a pleasantry had she not felt there was a touch of malice in his voice. 'I'm sure I can manage with a cushion, Dr Maddison,' she replied sweetly. 'Though I thank you for your offer.'

His grey eyes met hers steadily for a moment, and Gena felt a curious tremor pass through her. Perhaps it was the nervous anticipation of future battles.

The morning had been spent profitably for Gena, and had served to make her feel more at home. There was much here that was different from the hospital she was used to, but mostly the differences lay in the absence of technology. The process of examining, diagnosing and caring for sick people was the same. Incredibly, there was an old X-ray machine here, supplied secondhand in some period when the Health Authority was flush with funds, but there was of course no radiographer. Richard Maddison had shown her how to operate it herself, emphasising that she should always wear the lead apron that would protect her from repeated doses of radiation.

Pathology was also largely do-it-yourself, though samples could be sent by plane to Khartoum for analysis at the hospital there or for further shipment to Nairobi. Anything urgent must be done in the small laboratory here, however, since the plane might or might not arrive and, if it did, the samples might or might not get to Khartoum in one piece. If they did, the results could be radioed to Udari, and Richard Maddison showed her how to use the ancient radio.

Gena had been prepared for most of these exigencies, and had already acquainted herself with how to perform the blood counts and malarial smears and cultures which she would need to do here, but which were performed magically by laboratory staff for doctors in Sydney hospitals. They had sat for a while on stools in the laboratory with a quite decent microscope on the bench between them.

'This is a malarial slide,' said Richard. 'Study it. You'll see a lot of these.'

She bent her golden head to the eye-piece to identify the microscopic parasites in the red blood cells, till now only seen in books. There they were! She gave an exclamation of wonder, and raised her face excitedly to him. 'They're just like the textbooks!'

He looked back, unsmiling. 'The slides, yes. But the cases often aren't. So beware—they can fool

you.' He put another slide in the microscope.
'What's this one?' he asked.

Gena focused the instrument. 'Bilharzia,' she said.
'And this?'

Again she peered into the small circle of light at
organisms magnified many times. 'Trypanosomes—
sleeping sickness.'

'Good,' said Richard. 'Now look at this.'

She looked at yet another slide. Her voice was
uncertain. 'I don't see any organisms here. But there
aren't many red blood cells in this drop of
blood. . .lots of white cells. Too many. And hardly
any red.' She looked up at him.

'So what is it?' he demanded.

She frowned. 'It looks like leukaemia.'

'You're right,' said Richard. 'Don't ever forget.
They get all the Western diseases too.'

He took her to see the patients. There were
officially fifty beds in the small hospital, most of
which were full all the time. At times, however, they
cared for a hundred patients here, laying them on
rush mats on floors and verandas.

There were so many children. Sick, miserable,
half starved but resigned, they touched Gena to the
point where she had to hold back her tears. She
examined some of them, Richard others. She
noticed Richard spoke to his patients softly and
comfortingly in their own language, often kneeling
on the floor so that his face was level with their own.

Gena knew no words of their tongue, but her blue
eyes and yellow hair appeared to speak a universal

language. One after another they smiled, all but the sickest of them, and reached out brown hands to touch her hair. Gena smiled back, stroking in turn their velvety dark brown skins, giving the comfort of body-talk.

One small boy hooked his skinny brown arms around her neck and rested his wasted cheek against hers, smiling and saying, 'Ee-ee.' He wouldn't let her go. She looked up at Richard helplessly, her eyes alight with laughter.

'I'll have to stay here,' she said, 'or bring him with me.'

Richard looked impatient. 'We'd better go—we'll be late for lunch,' he said brusquely. He turned on his heel and walked away, leaving Gena to extricate herself and follow.

Well, the chief doctor of Udari was certainly not a very friendly man, Gena reflected as she ran over the events of the morning in her mind. And, she began to feel, not even a very nice man, except with his patients. She had to admit he was different with them.

Over lunch, Richard made plans for the week. 'I'll go back to Kepa with Jonathan,' he was saying, addressing himself to Angus. 'You can stay here and help Dr Lamb settle in.'

Gena wasn't sure there wasn't some irony in his tone. His expression was completely neutral. She noted that he hadn't called her Gena yet, and somehow was unable to suggest it to him.

'Follow Dr Cameron's instructions,' he said to her. 'Learn from him. We'll probably be gone a week.'

The next week was one that Gena would always remember. It was the week in which she fell in love with Africa—with its harsh landscape, its gentle people, its fascinating creatures. After each long day in the hospital, when the sun had hidden itself behind the western horizon and a cool stillness settled over the vast continent, she would take a walk in a different direction—towards the mysterious Nuba Hills, down to the town of thatch and timber and tin huts, to the wadi in the west where an antelope might come to drink, to the clump of baobab trees where strange small insects scratched out a living.

In the evenings after dinner, if she was not needed in the wards, she would sit on the veranda swapping life histories with Angus and Heather and Matron, with Gudwe often lingering on the stone step laughing at their strange ways and telling of the ancient ways of the Atema. Sometimes Pauline was there, but she refused to be drawn into the conversation, sitting just outside the circle of the light, watching the others.

There was something odd about her, thought Gena—the quiet intensity, the sense of tension, like a waiting leopard, taut, ready to spring. She had noticed in the first day how Pauline's eyes followed

Richard, with a devotion that was clearly readable. Perhaps the poor girl was just in love, thought Gena.

She knew how that felt. There was time now, alone in her room at night, for the full realisation of what she had done to hit her. She longed for Peter—for his familiar arms about her, his lips in her hair, for the joy of telling him all about this fascinating place. She found herself composing conversations with him in her head, and wept to realise they would never occur. Never did she wish to reverse her decision, however, and it left her wondering how strongly she was able to love. For surely, had she loved him enough, she would have given up even this? Both Angus and Matron noticed at times that their new companion could become rather silent and sad. Elinor Potts forbore to probe these silences, sensing some loss. Angus, however, with the obtuseness of his type, blundered straight on to the subject.

'You haven't told us about your young man yet,' he said heartily one evening. 'Stands to reason—fine girl like you, must be a young man in the offing.'

Gena was silent for a moment. Well, they're becoming my friends, she thought. I may as well tell them. 'There was one,' she said, concentrating on keeping her voice steady. 'We parted just before I came here.' Try as she might, it was impossible to keep her voice from dropping a little at the end of that bald sentence.

Angus was not deaf to the emotion his question had called up. 'By Jove,' he said gruffly, 'didn't mean to pry, my dear. Dashed sorry—wouldn't upset you for the world.' He looked distressed.

Gena smiled at his evident concern. 'It's all right, Angus. I'm glad I told you. After all, you are my friends.'

The kind-hearted fellow beamed. 'Of course we are, my dear. Felt it at once. Firm friends—knew we would be.' He patted her knee, then sat back quickly, seeming to be rather surprised at himself.

It was easy to like Angus Cameron. He had a patient, cheerful way with the people which elicited trust, and a never-failing good humour with the staff. At the end of a week, Gena felt she had known him all her life. He was appreciative of her work, giving praise freely, helping in a kindly way, so that she felt free to do her best, to make suggestions and to take on responsibility for patients.

Matron too was easy to work with. She watched the new doctor at first, then having satisfied herself that Gena was competent and careful and knew when to ask for help, she relaxed and turned her vigilant eye back to the nursing staff. For these girls, native girls from the surrounding country, she was the sergeant-major. No transgression or omission escaped her eagle eye, and many a girl was seen to roll her eyes at the thought of Matron's wrath brought down on her head for a job left undone or not done with the same degree of competence as it would have been in London. Not that Matron was unkind—quite the reverse. But accept sloppy work she did not.

Heather called her 'the X-ray Eye' and seemed almost serious when she said that Matron knew what you were doing as long as you were within a five-mile radius. With Heather, Gena had developed an easy if superficial camaraderie. The older girl had been in the Sudan a year now, and was therefore a good source of information about the patients and the way things were done. She knew how Richard liked things done especially, and gave such information to Gena with a wealth of careful detail. She had reason to know, Gena learned; she had trained as a junior nurse under Richard Maddison in London.

Pauline Hickey remained aloof—an enigma. She rebuffed all Gena's efforts at friendship, maintaining the utmost formality, and continued to watch with a brooding expression.

Gena and a nurse called Mia battled all one night to deliver a young mother of her twins, the second of which was coming feet first. Angus had looked in at times, when his work would allow, but could see that where obstetrics were concerned Gena knew what she was doing. Similarly, Matron had kept an eye on the work of the African nurse, but finally decided that she was doing an excellent job under Gena's direction. She retired, with instructions to send for her if necessary.

Abuta, the mother, laboured bravely in the African position, kneeling much of the time. But she grew tired as the hours passed and the second twin refused to negotiate its way to the outside world.

'Abuta, I have to help this baby come,' said Gena. 'Can you tell her that, Mia?'

Mia translated for the mother, who answered quickly, her eyes on Gena's face.

'What did she say, Mia?'

'She says she trusts you, Dr Gena. She knows you make it all right.'

Gena looked back to Abuta and saw that it was true. There showed in her eyes, along with the pain, her faith that Gena would help her and her baby.

'OK, Mia, lay her on her back. I'm going to do something I've never done before. I've seen it done a number of times, though, and I'm damn well going to do it.'

With sweat pouring from her face and aching from the effort of maintaining her position, Gena one by one repeated the procedures she had been shown by Dr Julian, obstetrician at the Royal William, to expedite the delivery of babies coming feet first. As she worked, she murmured encouragement, words that Abuta could not understand, but which might comfort none the less by their tone. Occasionally she glanced at the girl, and was moved to see the mingled pain and trust there. She had to do it.

And finally she knew the joy of feeling cupped in her gloved hand one small foot, and then another, which she drew down, the little brown body following. And at last there was a small brown head with curly black hair, whose first act in the world was understandably to protest. Abuta cried now for the first time, but was smiling too, and reaching for her

child. And when the baby was cleaned and dried
and placed, wrapped up, in her mother's arms, Gena
found to her surprise that her own cheeks were wet
as well.

As they cleaned up the room, Abuta spoke to Mia
in Atema. Gena looked at the nurse, who smiled a
broad white smile at her.

'What is it?' Gena asked.

'She says do not be angry. She like to call the baby
Gena.'

Gena found it hard to speak, and found tears
welling afresh in her eyes. 'You tell her I'm not
angry, I'm honoured.'

Abuta seemed to understand.

It was three o'clock when Gena, with tired step,
crossed the stretch of grass from hospital to
residence. At the sound of her tread on the veranda,
a figure uncurled itself from a wicker chair.

'Gudwe!' said Gena in surprise. 'What are you
doing here?'

Gudwe grinned in the dark, his teeth white.
'Sleeping. You want something to eat now. You do
good job. In the hills they die—woman and baby
both. I got some food here. One minute only.'

Gena was touched. She murmured her gratitude.

It was true what he said, of course. In the hills
where Abuta came from, both she and the baby
would have perished.

'Here,' Gudwe said, dumping a plate in her hands
with his usual lack of ceremony. He smiled good-
night and slid noiselessly down the steps.

CHAPTER FOUR

IN THE morning it became obvious to Gena that she had many new friends in Udari. She had been too tired to wonder the night before how Gudwe had known what was happening almost before it was over. Now she marvelled at the efficiency of the bush telegraph, as she was greeted by patients and relatives with new warmth and with references to 'Dr Gena's baby'.

When the cool came to the land that evening, it was a tired but happy Gena who took her walk towards the wadi. The night seemed specially lovely. Or was it just that the people of Udari were becoming her friends, and the staff at the hospital a sort of family? The way to the wadi was familiar now, and the still water and the sounds of the bush. She was not afraid of being out here alone in the gathering dusk.

Beyond the wadi was a grassy plain and, further, a clump of trees—acacia trees. They had those in Australia. Gena walked across the plain towards the line of trees that in her country were called wattle. Gaining the trees, she sat down and leant against a dark, slim trunk. They smelled the same.

Perhaps she was dreaming of her own country; perhaps, tired, not thinking at all, but Gena didn't hear the man approaching across the dry ground. It was not until he stood before her, the moonlight gleaming on the butt of a rifle, that she saw him, and leapt to her feet with a gasp.

He shot out a hand and gripped her arm strongly, and in that moment she saw his face. 'Richard!' she gasped with relief. 'You frightened me, appearing like——' She didn't finish.

He pulled her roughly towards him, the grip on her arm hurting. 'What the hell do you think you're doing sitting out here a mile from anywhere by yourself?' His voice was rough and angry.

Her smile froze. 'I—shouldn't I be?' she asked.

He made a small noise of impatience and derision. 'Have you ever seen a human half eaten by a hyena?' he demanded.

Gena's scalp prickled and she shivered. 'I—I didn't think they'd come this close to civilisation,' she said in a small voice.

'You didn't think at all.' His tone was uncompromising.

Gena felt a wave of shame and embarrassment flood her. What a fool she'd been! And a nuisance. And what if there had been a hyena? She trembled inwardly at the thought of death creeping up on her on four noiseless paws in the darkness. The feeling of Richard Maddison's commanding hand on her arm wasn't that bad, she decided.

They walked in silence across the grasslands. Dark had come in earnest now and the studded dome of the sky arched over them. Gena turned her face towards those cool bright stars, and stumbled over a hillock of grass. The man's strong hand steadied her.

'There's a woman in the town you can have a look at,' he said now, in a low voice. 'She was attacked by one. Half her face was eaten.'

An involuntary cry of horror escaped her.

'Not the way I'd like to send you home to your parents. There are also old wells out here, hidden in the grass. You might not enjoy lying in the bottom of one with your leg broken.' His voice was full of sarcasm, and it came to Gena that he thought she was a foolish child who should never have left home. His next words confirmed it. 'The next time you do anything this stupid, I will be sending you home.'

Half an hour later Gena was in her room, and seething with resentment. Her homecoming had been distinctly humiliating.

'Ah, brought the Lamb back to the fold, eh?' Angus had joked on seeing them.

But Richard hadn't responded to his friend's humour. 'Do you know where she was?'

Angus had rightly seen this as a rhetorical question.

'A mile away—at the acacias!'

Angus's eyebrows had shot up. 'Damn me,' he'd said. 'I didn't know she was going that far.'

'Yes, I'm inclined to damn you too, Angus,' was Richard's reply.

Gena understood what he meant, and hadn't liked it at all. 'I'm responsible for myself!' she'd said, anger beginning to grow in her. They were treating her like a toddler who'd wandered away. 'I don't need anyone to nursemaid me,' she had added.

'It seems you do, Dr Lamb,' Richard had said coldly. 'And a damned nuisance it is.'

Flinging herself on her bed, Gena fumed. How rude he had been! How unpleasant! And unfair. She hadn't known. He had only to tell her and she would never make the same mistake again. There was no need for him to speak to her and about her like that. It was humiliating! He treated her like a child, and she wasn't a child. She was a fully qualified doctor, a responsible adult.

But she was a woman, she thought suddenly. Perhaps that was it. Richard Maddison didn't like female doctors. Females were OK as nurses. That was their natural role—to do as male doctors said. But not as medical colleagues.

It was the only explanation Gena could think of to account for the antipathy she had felt to be there from the start. If that wasn't it, then he just didn't like her. And, for some reason, she found that a very distressing thought.

When Gena returned to the hospital later to check on one of the children, Jonathan was there, as she had thought he would be. The two had only just arrived back from their patrol, and had brought two small patients with them.

He greeted her with evident joy. 'Lovely to be back with you, my dear girl,' he said.

'Didn't you enjoy your trip?' Gena asked. She was dying to go on one herself.

'One doesn't enjoy a patrol with Richard Maddison,' he declared. 'You'll know that yourself soon. One endures it.'

'He's not the friendliest man I've ever met,' said Gena casually. 'Is he always so abrupt and—and grim?'

'Only with those of whom he disapproves.'

She gave a short, mirthless laugh. 'I think I qualify.'

'Almost sure to,' said Jonathan matter-of-factly. 'Young, female, attractive—that means unsuitable.'

'That's not fair!' she protested. 'You can't judge people like that!'

'You're right, it's unfair,' he replied consideringly. 'But it gives us an unbreakable bond. I'm unsuitable too.' He grinned.

Gena laughed. 'Oh, well, that's a consolation, anyway.'

'I hoped it would be,' said Jonathan.

'What have we here?' she asked, surveying the two brown children in cots at the end of the ward, away from the other children.

'Ah,' said Jonathan, moving towards them, and indicating the children with his hand. 'Measles number one, and measles number two.' They looked sick, and miserable.

'Poor little things,' she said. 'Don't their mothers come too?' Many patients in the hospital were accompanied much of the time by relatives. It was the African way, and it wasn't discouraged. Mothers even slept beside their children at night, lying on grass mats on the floor. They helped care for them, bathing them, feeding them, persuading them to take their medicine.

Jonathan shook his head. 'Their mothers have other children to feed. And it's really very difficult for them to be spared from their village. The women are responsible for so much of the work out there. Anyway, in this case their mothers may not have had measles themselves, so if they haven't got it yet, it's better that they keep away and don't get it. Adults die from it too.'

Gena took this in. 'What are we going to do for them?' she asked.

He shrugged. 'Nothing specific, as you know. Just try to keep them alive till the illness has run its course—intravenous fluids, treat the fever. What we hope is that they don't get the brain involvement— measles encephalitis—or the pneumonia. They often do, of course. They seem to have little defence against it.'

They must be so frightened, Gena thought. 'Don't we immunise against measles?' she asked.

'Oh, yes, we try. The people in the town are immunised. But the vaccine is expensive and hard to get, and the Africans are doubtful about having it. So we haven't immunised very widely yet.'

'That means the people in this area won't get it, anyway.'

'That's right,' said Jonathan.

'Then we could get a couple of girls from the town here to act as surrogate mothers. To be here all the time. The nurses can't do that—there are too many patients.'

Jonathan considered it. 'Yes, we could. And it might help. Sometimes one feels that children die here because they feel abandoned and simply give up.' He thought some more. 'Adolescent girls, perhaps, who don't have children or too much responsibility yet.'

'I'll talk to Mia,' said Gena. 'She's from the town here.'

'We'd better talk to the boss about it too,' said Jonathan wryly.

So it was that Measles One and Measles Two, or Rejo and Ate, acquired an Udari mother apiece for their stay in the hospital. The Atema seemed to be interested in the idea, and to think it was right. And the girls who were assigned to the job appeared to be delighted. Gena wondered that it hadn't been done before.

With all four doctors at Udari, the pace of work slowed, and she had time to write to her parents, to read textbooks and to get to know Jonathan better. He was really a very amusing companion.

'Why did you come out here?' she asked him one day.

'Unhappy love-affair,' he replied with a mock solemnity that made her laugh.

'I don't believe you.'

'Adventure?' he offered.

She considered him, smiling. 'Maybe.'

'You wouldn't believe it was high-minded idealism, I suppose?' With a wry face, Gena shook her head, and Jonathan sighed. 'Nobody takes me seriously.'

She laughed again. 'Come on—the truth!'

'The old man,' he said. 'He wouldn't let me join his practice till I'd done something "useful".'

'Your father?'

'Yes. Though I have my doubts,' he told her conspiratorially. 'I think I may be a cuckoo in the nest, you know. There was a particularly charming gardener at one stage. . .'

CHAPTER FIVE

GENA was sorry when, after four days of having the team all together, Jonathan and Angus left with two trucks and a number of native helpers for El Adir in the west, where they would treat members of the Hamar tribe, camel herders who wandered north in the wet season to the edge of the grassland and south again when the water dried up on the Sahel.

And now that they were only two, the work intensified. There were new admissions from the town, and a few discharges. People got better or worse, or died. An Arab trading truck, laden with all sorts of cheap goods and presenting an incredible appearance, drew up outside and brought them a patient, a teenage boy who had been found dying of thirst and starvation on the route to Khartoum from El Adir. He had been walking to the town to look for work. His family were starving, the father was sick and the camels had died.

Yes, the Arab had confirmed, he had seen the hospital trucks. They would pass by this boy's camping place. But—shrugging his shoulders—what could they do? The camels were dead, and it was the camels that were important, not the dying father. Camels in the Arab Sudanese economy were the mainstay of life. If there was nothing else you could drink their milk.

The Nuba babies were still there. Measles Two was much better, and could go home as soon as the next patrol went to the hills. Measles One—Rejo— had not picked up, though they had fed him fluids into his veins to cure his dehydration. He was still lethargic and sick. The little Atema girl who was his 'mother' sat almost constantly by his side and crooned to him, magical songs to make him well.

Gena began to see the possible flaw in her surrogate mothering plan. Worried, she said so to Richard. 'Perhaps I shouldn't have started this thing with the girls. Mali seems to be growing so attached to him. If he should die. . .'

Richard thought, and answered finally, 'No, I think it's a good idea. We should have thought of it before. If there's one thing that the people of the Sudan are used to dealing with, it's death—even the young ones. Mali has seen younger brothers and sisters die, and neighbours' children and strangers. She'll grieve, because they're loving people. But she knows that sick children die, and she'll cope if Rejo does.' He turned to her and appeared to examine her face. 'Perhaps better than we will,' he added.

Gena found it difficult working with Richard Maddison. He was distant and formal, communicating with her in a brusque manner that bordered on the rude, and sometimes passed the boundary. He never smiled and gave little encouragement. The comfort she had known with Angus, the easy camaraderie, was gone.

It was there, of course, with Matron, who often

helped her with some tricky task, but the flow of her easy chatter with Elinor Potts seemed to dry up when Richard appeared, and she became silent and nervous and, to her annoyance, awkward. It soon seemed to Gena that nothing would go right with Richard watching. Intravenous lines would not go in easily as they normally did; ampoules of drugs would shatter in her hands; she would inevitably touch something unsterile during a sterile procedure and have to use another of their precious stock of surgical gloves.

Richard said nothing in response to these difficulties, but she was certain he was thinking her a fool. The more she tried not to confirm his bad impression of her, the more she seemed to make mistakes. She grew afraid to give her opinion on diagnosis and treatment in case she should say something thoughtless and ignorant. And she was, after all, a very junior doctor compared with Richard Maddison.

If only he would go away, she thought. But that would be awful too. She didn't feel prepared to be left alone to care for all these sick people. The thought that he was always there to turn to was comforting even if he was unfriendly and impatient.

'You must have an opinion, Dr Lamb. Say what you think,' he said, frowning down at her at the bedside of an old woman she had asked him to see.

'W-well, I think she's in heart failure—I'm not sure why. She came in with pneumonia.'

And Richard quickly bent down to examine the woman, speaking softly and reassuringly to her, watching her face and smiling as he moved the stethoscope over her chest and listened. With a few final words to the woman and a press of her hand, he stood up.

'Yes, she is. If you listen very carefully, you'll hear a murmur. She has rheumatic heart disease, which is very common here. It probably didn't trouble her till the infection in her lungs put an extra load on her heart.'

Gena had to admit he was an excellent doctor. And she was learning an enormous amount.

If only he didn't keep watching her! She would be chattering away with the nurses or the patients, picking up the local language in leaps and bounds now, and enjoying her work, when all at once she would be aware of him. He would stand at the foot of the bed, tall and silent, watching her with an expression she found unfathomable on his good-looking face but which she thought was probably mistrust. For why should he be so often found watching her if he trusted what she was doing? Gena resented it. Junior and inexperienced she might be, compared to the others, but she knew when to ask for help. She didn't need to be supervised like a child.

Like a child! she thought again, with indignation. And the scene at the acacias and afterwards came back to her, with a fresh wave of resentment.

She often had to ask for his help, especially with the children. Gena's paediatric training had been limited so far, and, in any case, things were different out here.

'I'll have to ask Dr Maddison to look at this little fellow, Matron,' she decided.

They had just received a new patient, a baby with serious dehydration, who seemed from the way he drew up his legs and screamed from time to time to have a tummyache. There was gastroenteritis in his village. There always was, Gena reflected, in every village. But this seemed a little different.

Summoned to the bedside, Richard replied to Gena's explanation with a grunt. It flashed through her mind for a moment that perhaps his communication style made him ineligible for a Harley Street practice, and she grinned to herself at the thought. She knew it was unjust, however. He communicated perfectly well with the patients.

He was bending down now and murmuring soothingly to the baby, feeling his little tummy.

Presently another wave of pain seemed to come to the child. He doubled up his legs and screamed with it. Richard let his hand rest lightly on the upper abdomen. At length it seemed to go away and the child seemed happy again. Richard straightened up.

'A crying child with no tears,' he rapped. 'What does that mean?'

'Serious dehydration,' Gena replied.

He gave a grunt in reply, as though to say, she thought, Well, at least you know that.

'And a baby who cries in pain periodically, and looks quite happy between bouts?' He turned to look at her, and the full force of his clear grey eyes on hers brought that feeling of electrification she had known before. Was it fear? It was the strangest feeling, and wholly disconcerting. It made her heart thud.

'Come on!' he said impatiently.

'I-It's—some sort of colic,' she stumbled. 'But not—it's unusual for gastroenteritis. I wonder if it's pyloric stenosis.'

'Then put your hand here and wait,' he said, indicating the spot on the baby's abdomen over the pylorus—the junction between stomach and intestine.

She did so. And presently, when the next wave of pain came, she could feel a lump, the size and shape of an almond, in the little brown belly.

She looked up. 'I can feel it,' she said. 'What will we do? Send him to Khartoum?'

Richard thought a moment, frowning. 'No,' he said finally. 'It's a simple operation to relieve the narrowing. With your assistance, I can do it here.'

It was the first time Gena had seen the operating theatre used for anything but minor procedures, and she felt a thrill of excitement as they scrubbed for the case a day later. In that day, the baby's dehydration and salt depletion had been corrected with intravenous fluids, closely supervised by Richard. There was a tube down into his stomach, emptying it out so nothing would have to negotiate the narrowed passageway from stomach to gut. Richard looked larger than ever in his green theatre gown, and his hands finely shaped, strong and supple in their gloves.

'You're the anaesthetist,' he said to Gena. 'The drugs are drawn up on the tray. I've checked the doses myself. You can put a tube in, can't you?'

She swallowed. 'I think so,' she said. She had put a few breathing tubes into children, but she wasn't experienced.

'You'd better be able to,' he growled. 'You've got three minutes once you've given the drugs. He can't breathe for himself then.'

Anxious and trembling, Gena somehow did it, while Richard stood there waiting, his eyes vigilant over his mask. The tube was connected to the oxygen and anaesthetic gas. Gena checked its position by listening to the baby's lungs. Yes, it was all right. The oxygen was getting down there.

'OK—scrub, and put gloves on, and come round this side of the table,' he told her. 'Matron will monitor him.'

Gena's job now was to stand beside Richard and hold the instruments that would draw the skin apart, so he could get into the pylorus. Pauline stood on the other side, ready to hand the instruments.

'Get in close to me,' he said. 'You can't do it from three feet away.' Gena moved closer. 'Close, I said!' His voice was irritable. 'Stand against the table, with me.'

She leant up against the table and felt her hip against his side.

'That's better,' he said. 'Now you can see what

you're doing. Take the retractors and pull back the skin of the incision.'

Gena stood there as he worked to expose the pylorus and make the incision that would relieve the obstruction. She had always felt slightly uncomfortable in the operating theatre, shoved up against some perspiring surgeon, both of them trying to get at the same small hole.

This was no different. Richard had turned towards her and the incision now, so that he was pressed against her side. His masked face hovered about her right ear, so that she could hear his even breathing as he concentrated on his task. His body felt warm against her, and for some reason she felt very strange. She knew she was breathing fast. It must be the heat. This theatre was not like the ones at home, which were like igloos in winter.

He glanced down at her. 'All right?' he enquired abruptly.

She met his eyes for a moment, then wished she hadn't as their clear grey gaze did their disconcerting thing again. What was it about his eyes? She supposed they embarrassed her.

Quickly she nodded in reply, and he resumed his work. But she was glad when the operation was over, with the baby's belly neatly sewn up and the tube taken out of his lungs, the child breathing on his own again.

Richard pulled off his mask, and the strong lines of nose and jaw, the decided mouth, were revealed again. 'Good work,' he said briefly, and stood for a moment looking at her, before reaching out gently to pull her forgotten mask from her face.

It was remarkable how two words of praise could cheer you, thought Gena later, as she kicked off her shoes in her little room and curled up in the sagging old armchair for a while. She felt positively light-hearted. Perhaps it was also the knowledge that the child would recover now. Such a life-saving operation! Soon he would be gaining weight and growing fit and strong. She felt a great glow of satisfaction, and an admiration for the skill of Richard Maddison, remembering his patient concentration and the sure movements of his graceful hands. He can take out my appendix any day, she thought. One might not like him, he might be surly and impatient and rude, but one could trust him.

And surly, impatient and rude he continued to be. If anything, Gena thought, he was worse after the day of the operation than before.

With a sigh she concluded that those two words of praise were all she was ever likely to hear from him.

Mealtimes would have been difficult affairs had it not been for the presence of Matron Potts and Heather and even Pauline Hickey. Richard Maddison showed no inclination to talk to Gena and she herself was happy to be ignored by him. On Sunday night he didn't appear for dinner, and Gena felt it was really the most congenial evening they'd had since Angus's and Jonathan's departure.

At nine o'clock, however, a nurse came across from the hospital for her. The doctor wanted her. It was clear that however many doctors Udari had, Richard Maddison would always be *the* doctor. Gena went across and found him with little Rejo in the children's ward, and could see immediately why Richard was here and not at dinner. The child was worse. His colour was somehow grey under the brown and he was coughing in paroxysms that racked his wasted little body. Between the fits of coughing he lay still, his eyes lustreless and sunken. Mali sat on her mat beside him, watching the doctor's face.

'He's got pneumonia,' Richard said without looking up. 'It could be simply from the measles virus, or it could be a bacteria—secondary. Do you understand?'

'Yes,' said Gena.

'I can't afford to throw away drugs. I've got to diagnose what's there and treat it precisely. We need to obtain some sputum from his airway and look at it under the microscope. I want your help.'

'Of course,' she said.

Half an hour later they had completed the difficult task of obtaining a sample of sputum from the airway of a small child, and Richard was making a slide from it, staining it with special stains to make any bacteria identifiable. He put the slide under the scope and looked, sitting back in a moment and motioning to Gena to put her eye to the piece.

'It looks like——' she began, but was cut off.

'Don't tell me what it looks like!' Richard snapped. Gena sat up in amazement, staring at him.

'Tell me what it is,' he said fiercely. 'You're a great one for saying "I think" and "It looks like", aren't you, Dr Lamb? Well, that's no good here. There's no laboratory, no pathologist here who can ring you up and say, "Yes, I confirm your thoughts on the subject, Doctor." There's nothing but you. And the patient's life will depend on your *knowing*; not thinking, or suspecting, or hoping. Do you understand?'

Gena nodded dumbly, a flush beginning to spread over her face.

'Then look again, Dr Lamb, and tell me what it *is*.'

She did as he said. She looked at the small round blue discs she saw gathered in clusters on the slide and compared them in her mind with other slides she had seen, with what she had learnt as a student. Finally she sat up.

'They're staphylococcus,' she said. 'A staphylococcal pneumonia.'

'Then let's treat it,' said Richard, rising. 'And hope we're in time.'

Back in the ward, they went to work silently to give Rejo the drugs, straight into his veins, that they prayed would kill the microbes colonising his little lungs. They put a mask with oxygen on his small face, placed a fan by his bed to bring down the fever which had climbed again with the new infection, then sent a reluctant Mali home to bed.

'You go,' said Richard to Gena, and she did as she was bidden, without a word.

On the veranda of the silent house she sat alone, his words in the lab reverberating in her ears. 'I think', 'It looks like'! Such contempt in his tone! She felt the tears springing to her eyes. I hate him, she thought. I've never hated anyone before, but I hate him. He loves to humiliate me.

Richard's footsteps on the gravel path made her stiffen, then hurriedly wipe her face on her sleeve. Slowly he mounted the veranda steps and, glancing in her direction, collapsed wearily into a chair. He stared silently straight ahead of him.

'I can't do any more by sitting there,' he said at last, dully—and seemed to be about to lapse into silence again, till he turned suddenly to face her and say, with an agony in his voice that Gena had not guessed at, 'Do you know what it's like to leave a village with two children, and only bring one back?'

She looked away. The pain in his face made her feel ashamed. And of course she hadn't considered it. The two mothers waiting, the one child carried from the truck. . .it was awful! And he would be the one to take the one child back. Suddenly she longed to comfort him, and turned to him again to reach her hand out.

It was too late. He had got up, and said, 'Good-night,' in quite an ordinary voice.

CHAPTER SIX

IN THE morning Gena awoke with the night-time coolness already ebbing away. She rose, washed, dressed, and as she did thought about Richard Maddison.

What a contradiction the man was! So fine a doctor, so tender and thoughtful with his patients. And with her—rude, overbearing, arrogant, unfair. Yes, unfair, for hadn't he disliked her on sight? And kept to that opinion, no matter what she did. A part of Gena pleaded on his behalf. He was right in what he'd said—she had to know, not think.

And he had, of course, been motivated by concern for his patient.

The other part of Gena scoffed. Rot! it said. There was no need for him to make his point so cruelly. He was motivated equally by his sheer dislike of her. It was hard to forgive him.

She went to breakfast with mixed feelings. Richard was already there, and had clearly been up some time. Gena looked at him expectantly. 'Rejo?' she asked, fearing the answer.

He glanced up. 'Better,' he said briefly.

She gave a sigh of relief. 'Oh, Richard!' she exclaimed. 'I'm so glad!' and was, for him and the child. She waited for him to say more.

But he didn't. He simply gave the briefest grunt and continued to read his journal, not even raising his eyes again. It turned her off her breakfast.

But Gudwe wasn't having that. 'Eat. Eat!' he chided her. 'You want to be skinny always? Eat!'

It made Gena laugh, and that made her feel a lot better.

That morning Angus and Jonathan came home, much to her joy. It was so much nicer when they were there. Even so, it was hard to throw off a little cloud of depression, and Jonathan was quick to notice.

He made a face at her, pulling down the corners of his mouth. 'I don't suppose you could bring yourself to look genuinely happy at our arrival?' he asked, and made her grin at least.

'You don't know how happy I am,' she said fervently. 'Aha!' he cried, and pretended to examine her face closely. 'I see the signs of a week spent alone with Richard Maddison. The new lines on the face, the haggard look, the hair prematurely grey.'

She laughed in earnest now. 'Don't be ridiculous,' she said. 'It wasn't that bad.'

'You don't have to be brave with me, my dear,' he said. 'I understand. Even Angus has noticed it, you know, and he doesn't notice much.'

'Oh, don't, Jonathan,' she protested. 'Angus is the dearest man.'

And Angus had noticed it, and come to his own conclusions about its source. He had mentioned it to Richard in his gruff way.

'I think young Gena could do with some cheering up, Richard. You going to the Nuba Mountains this week?'

'Yes,' Richard answered, frowning. 'Those children with the measles should be right by the end of the week. I'll take them back and then push on towards Kosti. See some of the people to the north there.'

'Why don't you take her with you? Take her mind off things.'

Richard raised an eyebrow. 'What things?' he asked.

Angus looked embarrassed. 'Shouldn't say too much,' he said, rubbing his head doubtfully. 'Told in confidence.' He hesitated, then went on, 'Fact of the matter is, she had something of a disappointment before she came here. Parted from some young chap. Gets a bit down in the dumps at times.'

Richard curled his lip. 'Yes, that explains her presence here. Typical romantic idea!' His voice was contemptuous. 'Disappointed in love, so they volunteer to work in Africa. Like joining the Foreign Legion. The worst possible reason for anyone to come here.'

'My dear chap,' Angus was protesting, 'that's not it at all. I'm sure.'

'You're rather too partial to see things as they are, my friend,' said Richard. 'Anyway,' he got up, 'there's work to do. Let's go.'

And Angus followed him across to the hospital,

still shaking his head, but unable to find the words to convince his friend he was wrong.

But Richard did let Gena accompany him on the next patrol. At the end of the week, young Rejo's pneumonia had completely cleared and he was gaining weight. It was time to take the two infant boys back to their home in the hills, back to the families who still prayed to the Nuba gods for their survival.

There was a hundred kilometres of track between Udari and their destination. It was not a good enough surface to be called a road, but it was better than most tracks in the Sudan, and they should be able to accomplish the trip in a day if all went well. They would check the villages when they got there for further problems, and spend a day or two winding their way through the hills. After that, there would be a short patrol to the north towards Kosti, though not that far. Medical teams from Khartoum went out to see the people of Kosti itself.

The road from the Nuba hills to Kosti was another matter. The further north the track wound, the deeper the drifts of sand and the more difficult it became to follow the way at all. Richard had done it many times, however, and knew what he needed to take with him to ensure their successful return.

'Now you watch out for the hyenas,' Heather told Gena at dinner the night before. 'Stay close to everyone. We don't want you to be eaten.'

Gena made a face. 'Are there lots up there?'

'Plenty,' said Heather emphatically. 'I've been on patrol up there, and you always hear them.'

She'd wondered if the nursing staff went on patrol. Angus said they did sometimes, but with the hospital as it was their labour was needed here. It was one reason for hiring another doctor. Matron was happy she didn't have to spare a nurse, but Heather, Gena thought, would clearly have liked to be going. She gave Gena instructions as to what Richard would expect and what should be done to help him with such detail that Gena began to feel impatient. Richard obviously had no trouble inspiring loyalty in the nursing staff, she reflected. Or perhaps, as with her, it was fear.

They would not, on this trip, be taking African helpers. It was a long haul, and they needed to carry extra supplies of fuel and water and medicines. And Rejo and Ate would be carried in the back. There wasn't room for an extra body.

Even the prospect of a week spent in the exclusive company of Richard Maddison couldn't dampen Gena's enthusiasm for this expedition. For now she would see the real Africa—Africa as it had been and, in the remoteness of those distant hills, still was.

When she awoke in the morning it was with the same sort of feeling that children had on Christmas morning. At first she couldn't recall why she should be awake at five o'clock with a tingling of excitement in her. Then she remembered—they were going on patrol—and she felt a fresh wave of exhilaration and pleasure. But it was only five o'clock. So, as she had on all those Christmas mornings of her childhood, she tried to contain her anticipation and go back to sleep to make the time till the magic moment go faster.

It was no good. At five-thirty, she gave it up and at quarter to six was eating her breakfast in the cool of a perfect African morning.

As early as it was, Richard Maddison had preceded her. She could see him through the window in the grey light, stowing boxes in the truck parked in the residence yard. Gudwe was helping him. Breakfast done, she went out to see if she could help.

Richard cocked an eyebrow when he saw her. 'You're up early,' he remarked.

'What can I do to help?' she asked.

'Nothing,' he answered shortly. 'Just get your gear, and we'll stow it.'

If Gena was excited about her journey, she was not alone. For two small Africans, now well enough to be fascinated by all the new things around them and delighted at the prospect of a ride in a truck, it was also a very special day. Rejo and Ate were going home to their village, and Richard made a comfortable seat for them in the back with boxes and rugs, and lifted them in.

By then the other inhabitants of the residence had appeared. Matron was there to offer last-minute advice, and Heather to remind Gena again of the hyenas. Angus gave her a giant hug and Gudwe warned her, 'Wear that hat,' and, 'Drink plenty water.' She promised faithfully to drink plenty of water, wear her hat and avoid hyenas.

Jonathan had a few private words to say. 'Keep your spirits up, my girl. Your ordeal will soon be over!'

Gena laughed guiltily, looking to see whether Richard had heard, but although he was looking their way, he was out of earshot.

Jonathan went on solemnly, 'And if the truck breaks down and it looks as though you'll be out there forever with him, I advise you to administer yourself a fatal dose of something.'

Laughing again, Gena hugged him, then climbed up into the cabin.

At seven the truck's engine first rattled, then roared into life. Their colleagues waved them off from the steps of the residence, and a farewell party of native children ran alongside, calling and laughing, till they cleared the hospital gates. Rejo and Ate, sitting in the back, waved and called back, their eyes shining large with pleasure.

Gena sat upright in her seat, swaying with the motion of the truck over the uneven ground.

Richard glanced at her. 'You'd better get comfortable,' he said. 'You'll be sitting there for a long time.'

She looked into the back. The children seemed perfectly happy. She slid down in her seat a little, the seatbelt loose across her lap, and looked at the scenery.

When noon came, it was already beginning to

seem like a long journey. Gena had made herself as comfortable as possible by now, with her sleeping-bag stuck between the seat and her spine, and her bare feet braced against the dashboard. The truck bounced and shuddered over the sandy red track and the sun made it an oven on wheels. It was debatable whether it was best to have the windows up and suffer the heat, or put up with the red dust for the sake of the breeze their motion created. The children seemed to mind not at all, but sat up still with eyes as big as saucers, pointing things out to one another and laughing excitedly from time to time. Sparse grasslands and stunted shrub stretched out around them as far as one could see, and Richard had not spoken again.

Gena glanced at him covertly from time to time as he steered the lumbering vehicle along the road. Sweat already soaked his khaki shirt and gathered in beads on his forehead beneath the curling dark hair, but he looked perfectly at ease, gripping the wheel loosely with large brown hands and leaning one elbow on the window ledge. If he was thinking of anything but piloting the vehicle over the difficult road, he didn't share his thoughts.

At one o'clock, however, as they crested a rise in the road, he pulled off to one side and switched off the engine. Gena leaned forward and looked out of the window. Below them was stretched the sandy red plain they had traversed, and, very distantly now, the town of Udari and the hospital were a speck on that desolate expanse.

Richard stretched his long legs and arched his spine. 'Let's have lunch,' he said.

It was a suggestion that found instant favour with the boys, and Gena smiled with pleasure to see the agile way they climbed down from the back of the vehicle, well enough to refuse her help.

They sat on what existed of the grass on top of the hill, Richard leaning on one elbow, his long legs outflung, and Gena resting her back against the dusty wheel of the truck, in the shade of it. He continued to be uncommunicative, so she left him to his brooding silence and gave her attention to the children. It was good to see them eat so hungrily, especially Rejo, who had been so close to death. She hugged him when he thanked her for the food and he put both arms around her neck and hugged her back, his teeth showing white in his dark face.

The afternoon's travelling was more difficult than that of the morning. They descended from their hill into a valley where the sand lay more deeply on the track, and not half an hour had passed before the truck, in attempting to negotiate a sand-filled depression, had spun its wheels and refused to proceed any further. Richard switched the engine off without a word and opened the door. As Gena prepared to do likewise, he paused.

'Where are you going?' he demanded, and added curtly, before she could answer, 'Stay where you are.'

'I'll help you——' she began.

'Do as you're told!'

It had been an order. Gena stayed put, turning to watch as, from the back of the truck, he unpacked shovels and lengths of wood. She watched through the open door as he rolled his sleeves further up and began to dig the sand away from under the wheels.

It was slow work under a hot sun. For half an hour he toiled, the sinews standing out on his strong arms as he dug the shovel in and lifted the sand. In the truck, Rejo and Ate watched attentively, and Gena became increasingly impatient. Why should she stay here? It would be accomplished much more quickly if he let her help. She felt angry at him for scorning her assistance, and hot, and bored.

Finally, however, he had the boards in place beneath the wheels, and had thrown the shovel in the back and slammed the door. He started the engine, and gradually they moved forward on to firmer ground, where he stopped in order to recover the precious boards.

The treacherous valley traversed, they began to climb in earnest now into the Nuba Mountains. The road was reduced to a faint track which wound around rocks and shrubs, pitted by eroded gulleys and gutters through which the truck crawled, its engine protesting in a whine.

No one had exaggerated about the track, Gena reflected. It was terrible! But there were tracks like this in Australia, too, and she itched to have a go at driving the truck over them. A look at Richard's uncompromising profile, however, convinced her that she had better not suggest it. He wouldn't even let her help unbog them. She made a wry face to herself. If he only knew how many times she had unbogged a truck back home. . .

Rejo and Ate lived in the foothills of the mountains. Their people herded a few cattle and grew durra, or sorghum, the staple crop of the Sudan. It was only one day's drive from Udari, and as the sun fell towards the horizon, Gena knew they must be getting close.

The long day had taken its toll of the children at last, and they lay curled up in the back, oblivious now to the roar and whine of the engine and the rattling, bouncing ride. Gena longed for the journey to be over—for stillness and peace and, most of all, silence for a while; though, she reflected drily, there had been plenty of that from her colleague.

She wondered whether they would pass the entire patrol in this way. If so she might well lose the power of speech. There would be Africans to talk to, of course, with her limited but ever-growing vocabulary of Atema words. She hoped she might still be understood in spite of the regional variations, and that she might pick up a lot more on this trip.

Thinking in this vein, she was surprised when Richard did speak.

'It's through this pass and over the next rise,' he said, and she knew he meant the village.

And when they crested that rise, Gena could see it below them in the late afternoon sun—the collection of simple huts huddled together in an expanse of flat, sheltered ground, surrounded by fields of sorghum. And finally she saw the people. The entire village was assembled as Richard guided the truck along the last piece of winding track through the durra. They had been listening, of course, to the sound of the truck advancing for an hour.

Gena sensed instinctively that this was not the usual welcome. There was waving and greetings and smiles, but there was also a tension, a constraint— for two families waited to know whether this was a sorrowful day or a joyful one.

Richard did not delay. He climbed down from the truck and went to open the back where his two small patients were curled up sleeping. He lifted Rejo out first and carried him towards the waiting villagers, and suddenly there broke from a woman there a strangled cry as she darted forward to take her child. Rejo, awake now, clutched his little arms about her strongly.

But another mother waited. She was young, hardly more than a girl, and her large eyes were fixed on Richard Maddison with such a mixture of hope and fear that Richard reached out to her. She drew herself up as though to withstand a blow, but he spoke to her softly in her own language.

'Come,' he said. 'He is here.' He led her gently to the truck, and when she saw the child sleeping there, she covered her mouth with both hands and rocked herself back and forward in a little song of joy. Richard lifted him and he awoke, calling for his mother, 'Ame!'

And now the restraint in the village was gone, and

there was laughing and calling and hands reaching out to stroke Richard's shoulder in their traditional manner of greeting a friend. And they gave voice also to their astonishment and delight in his companion, who was a small, graceful creature with hair the colour of summer grass, and a girl. A crowd of people surrounded her, saying 'Ee-ee!' in their way and stroking her golden hair. One woman discovered the same fine golden hair growing on Gena's arms, and they all stroked it, exclaiming.

Laughing herself, Gena looked up and found Richard's eyes on her. He smiled faintly.

And now she understood what it was like for him to come back to these villages without the children he had borne away. They would not blame him, but she knew how much he would feel their grief. She wondered afresh what had made him choose this life—isolated, difficult, lonely—then she looked at the faces of the loving, intelligent people around her and felt she knew.

That evening they shared the food of the village. It was hard for Gena to reconcile taking their precious food when half the Sudan was starving, but she realised that this was part of their thanks, and that it gave them pride to offer it. There were several types of vegetables and a sort of cake made from durra, but Gena really felt too tired to be very interested. What she wanted was sleep.

Richard seemed to realise this. 'The tent's pitched,' he told her. 'Your things are up one end.

Go when you want, but don't wander far away for any reason.'

And as soon as it seemed polite, she did go, and gave her face and hands the briefest wash with water from the jerrycan before peeling off her clothes, pulling on a long T-shirt and crawling into her sleeping-bag. She didn't even hear Richard come in later and get into his bag at the other end of the tent. She had been long asleep by then, curled up comfortably with only her golden hair showing.

She woke up early, feeling as good as she always did out in the bush. There was something about sleeping under canvas in the quiet of the countryside that filled her with energy.

Outside, it was cool and dim still, with a faint breeze that stirred the sorghum and made her feel alive. She washed again beside the truck, a little more thoroughly, then dressed herself and ate some cereal, as the sun stole up above low hills and at length discovered her.

Richard emerged from the tent, buttoning up his shirt and running his hand through unruly curls.

'Morning,' Gena said cheerily. She was perched on the truck's front mudguard in the sun, swinging her legs and drinking tea. 'There's tea there.'

'Thanks,' he grunted, and she examined him surreptitiously, interested to know how he looked first thing in the morning. Still attractive, she thought, but a much wilder sort of attractiveness. His dark curls were tousled, his shirt half buttoned, and the dark shadow of his beard made his face appear more rugged. Gena was reminded once again of her image of the bull—male, powerful, undomesticated. He looked very nice, she thought, and admired his broad shoulders and powerful thighs as he squatted down to pour some tea.

She was largely unaware that she too looked very nice, but it was a fact appreciated by the Atema, both men and women, who after breakfast came to their 'clinic'. In white shorts and loose white T-shirt, tucked in, she looked neat and cool, but also very appealing. More than one of the Atema could be seen admiring her. Richard Maddison's eyes, too, swept over the form of his assistant, but gave no indication of what he thought about it.

At lunchtime they left the village and headed for a short distance down the road they had come by, then turned to traverse a sandy valley before continuing their climb into the hills. After only an hour's travelling, they found themselves bogged again in a drift of sand. This time Richard gave the smallest sigh before jumping out.

And this time Gena didn't ask if she could help. She merely pulled her boots back on, stuck her hat on her head and climbed down from the truck. He had already begun to dig away the sand, but he paused when he saw her.

'I thought I told you yesterday to sit in the truck,' he growled.

She eyed him evenly, then nodded. 'Yes, you did,' she said. 'But that was yesterday. And I'm not going to be a passenger on this trip.' She reached into the back of the truck and pulled out the other shovel, then, bending, dug it into the sand with a determination that seemed to silence him.

They worked, side by side, for twenty back-breaking minutes, Richard only stopping occasionally to glance at his small assistant, Gena not stopping at all.

At the end of that time, every board they had was stuck in the sand under the truck's wheels. They flung their shovels in the back and straightened up. Richard took his hat off and wiped his face with his arm, and contemplated his companion.

Gena was covered in red dust from head to foot. It had gathered deeply in the folds of her white shorts and shirt. The sweat which had rolled down her face had left tracks in it. Her blonde curls were powdered with it.

For a moment she saw that a small smile curved Richard's mouth as he looked at her. She grinned at him in return, her teeth showing white in her red face.

'This is OK,' she said. 'Back home it's mud.'

'Hm.' He made an uninterpretable sound, then added, 'Thanks for your help.'

They bogged the truck twice more before reaching that night's camping place. On these occasions, Richard didn't refuse her help, and, cheered with this acceptance, she worked good-humouredly and indefatigably towards digging them out. She offered to drive the truck forward as he rammed the boards in under the wheels, and found she hadn't lost her touch at driving a Land Rover, but rather skilfully eased it forward through the drifts, talking to it all the while.

'I must remember to do that,' said Richard as he climbed back into the driver's seat Gena had vacated. 'It obviously helps.'

'What?' she queried.

'Give the truck instructions,' he said drily.

On the last occasion, he let her dig for a while, then stopped her with a hand on her shoulder. 'Have a break,' he said, and added gruffly, 'You must be getting tired.'

It was the most kindly he had ever spoken to her, and Gena suddenly found herself thinking he mightn't be so bad after all. But she didn't give up on a job.

'I'll stop when this damn thing's out of here!' she declared, giving the truck an ill-tempered kick.

This time he grinned at her in earnest.

Tired was what she was, Gena had to admit to herself, when they finally drew in to a sheltered spot for the night. And dirty. She slid rather painfully from the truck to ease her cramped legs and hoped they carried enough water to have a decent wash tonight.

They did, and Richard poured some of it into a stainless steel bowl for her, tossed her some soap and announced his intention of taking a stroll. Gena guessed he was providing an opportunity for her to have some sort of bath, so when his tall figure was out of sight she stood at the back of the truck and stripped off her clothes. The water in the bowl was still warm from the heat of the day, but it felt wonderful to wipe off the dirt with a flannel. Finally she dangled her hair in it, then stood upright, letting it drip down all over her. A light breeze had arisen and cooled her now, caressing her wet body. Above her burnt the African stars. A great wave of contentment suddenly stole through her, and even her physical weariness felt pleasant. The crunch of Richard's step on the road brought her back to a sense of time and place, and she hastily towelled the remaining moisture off her and pulled on a clean T-shirt and jeans. She picked up her dusty clothes as he reappeared.

'Does the local laundry pick up and deliver?' she asked with mock seriousness, and was rewarded by a faint smile. 'Well, I guess it's my turn to go for a walk,' she said.

But he answered sharply, 'No, you stay in sight,' as he stripped off his shirt.

Gena stood for a moment, uncertain what to do, as he lifted the water can and poured more water, the muscles contracting in a nice way in his chest and shoulders. He had some hair on his chest, she noticed, just a little—fine and dark. And some more in a fine line on his belly, disappearing under his belt. His chest was perfect.

She turned away. Then she spied a convenient rock and sat on it with her back to him as he stripped off his remaining clothes and washed.

The flat rock made a good table, and they ate their dinner there. Gena was used to bush cooking and enjoyed the improvisation that it entailed. On the Primus stove she cooked a stew of her own devising, which she christened *Boeuf du Bog*, after the events of the day. Richard laughed at this, and, cheered by such unlooked-for success in entertaining her dour superior, she chatted to him a little as she cooked. She explained to him the art of baking a pudding in a billycan, an endeavour whose success he seemed to regard with a degree of scepticism until he tasted it.

'This is damned good,' he said with surprise, and Gena endeavoured to give him a withering look by lamplight. 'In fact,' he added, 'this would have to rank as the best dinner I've ever had in the bush.'

She looked up at him to see whether he was serious. He looked it. What an epoch-making day! she thought. He had thanked her for helping him, praised her cooking, shown concern for her weariness, and even smiled at her! More than once, she thought in wonder. Maybe she was winning him round. The thought was irresistibly exciting. Maybe she was getting there. Maybe, with effort and time, he was going to accept her.

Or maybe, said a cynical little voice, he just approved of the fact that she could cook—a traditional womanly skill. No, be fair, she told herself. He had let her help him with the truck, and thanked her for her efforts. He had come as close as he ever had to being friendly. Maybe he wasn't so bad once you got to know him.

Contemplatively, Gena ate her last mouthful of pudding, then was embarrassed to look up and find Richard surveying her silently. Their eyes met for a moment, his as unfathomable as ever, then he stretched out his long body on the ground and looked up at the sky.

'Clear night,' he remarked in his deep tones, and Gena followed suit, lying on her back and gazing at the brilliance above. They lay there side by side for a while, with the lamp turned down, listening to the noises of the night. It was inexpressibly peaceful, and for the first time Gena felt the silence between them to be companionable rather than strained.

At length, however, he sat up and gathered together their plates, saying quietly, 'We'd better get some sleep.'

Gena felt that nothing could keep her awake tonight. But she had reckoned without the hyenas. No sooner had she curled up gratefully in one corner of the roomy tent than she heard the hoarse cry on the breeze. She had never heard a hyena's call before, but no one had to tell her what it was. Nothing else could make that unearthly sound. She shivered in her sleeping-bag, and tried not to listen, or only to think of the beauty of the animal, not of what it could do. There was obviously no danger. They were inside a tent whose flap was secured, and Richard lay still in his corner, his breathing in the stillness even and slow. The call came again, and this time closer by. It sounded like a howl of death, long and spine-chilling.

Gena sat up, her heart thudding. She heard the small noise made by Richard turning to see what she was doing.

He seemed to know what she was feeling. 'They can't hurt you,' he said softly.

She took a deep breath. 'No,' she said. 'Only. . . I keep thinking. . .'

'It's my fault,' he said, surprisingly. 'I shouldn't have frightened you before.' It was true, she *had* been thinking of that woman. . . 'Come close to me,' he said, so low that at first she wasn't sure that she had heard right. But he sat up, and said more commandingly, 'Come here!' And outside, in the moonlight somewhere, the cat cried again.

Gena went.

His voice was close to her now. 'Lie across the tent,' he said, and she lay down in her sleeping-bag as he told her. He stretched out next to her, between her and the tent flap, just touching her.

'There,' came his voice in her ear. 'Now it'll have to eat me first.'

'Oh, that *is* a comfort,' said Gena in a small voice, and she felt his breath on her hair as he laughed.

'I had thought it *might* be,' he murmured, and she was uncertain whether there was irony in his tone.

'I don't think I'd want to be out here without you,' she confessed, and there was silence for a moment.

Then he said, so softly that she only just heard him, 'I'm here,' and surprisingly, she felt his big hand close around her small one. And the strength of it, its hardness and its very size, seemed to take away all her fear, as he must have known it would.

She closed her eyes, and in minutes was asleep.

When the morning sunlight penetrated the canvas of the tent sufficiently to awaken her, Gena was embarrassed to find herself huddled against Richard's side. The fears of the night seemed far away now, and she felt more than a little silly.

She sat up quietly to creep away, but found his eyes open and his gaze on her.

'Good morning,' he said briefly, and she looked for a sardonic expression in his face. But it seemed to hold no particular expression at all.

Breakfast over, they packed up and set off again, and since Gena had proved that she had some idea of how to handle a Land Rover, Richard let her drive. The plan was that she would take the first even stretch of track and hand the wheel over to him when the going got rough, but she was so obviously at home behind the wheel of the truck and so effortlessly guided it over the now rocky country that he raised no objection when she changed down into low gear to tackle the rising ground, and she drove till they stopped for lunch.

Richard was quiet again, and Gena found herself singing to herself to pass the time. She darted a glance in his direction when she discovered herself indulging in this lifelong habit, but he didn't seem to be objecting. He had stretched out his powerful frame as much as he could in the confines of the passenger's seat, and was gazing out of the window.

Nor did he demur when after lunch she climbed boldly into the driver's seat again and started the engine. It was Gena who regretted her decisiveness when she slowed down to change gear on a rocky slope and found the wheels uselessly spinning when she tried to accelerate. She jammed her foot on the brake and pulled on the handbrake.

'Damn!' she said, with which fairly moderate curse she put the truck in reverse and prepared to roll back down the steep slope.

Richard turned to survey the track with its precipitate drop to one side, gave Gena one long hard look, then turned back to the front with his arms folded. Slowly, with infinite concentration, Gena steered the truck back down to the bottom in reverse, and gave a sigh of relief.

'Sorry,' she said.

He looked at her with a glint in his eyes. 'Not at all,' he said evenly. 'Think how it would have hurt my pride if you'd managed to drive it all day without any bother!'

Gena gave a delighted laugh, and later, when she stalled it on another rutted slope, gave him to understand she was only protecting his pride by trying to even their score.

Midway through the afternoon, they arrived at their second village, a proper hill community that lived in a way little changed from that of the past.

They were not quite prepared for the advent of

Richard's driver, and words of greeting turned to the now familiar expressions of astonishment and delight, as she slid from behind the wheel and sprang to the ground.

But even an apparition as amazing as Gena could not entirely halt ceremony. A hush fell for a moment as a very old man approached Richard, held both arms wide and intoned a solemn speech in a language Gena had not yet heard. She watched as Richard, equally sombre, first bowed his head, then answered in the same language. Then a broad grin split the face of the old one, and the two men embraced, with which signal the general hubbub recommenced, and Gena found herself the centre of the usual crowd.

CHAPTER SEVEN

ALL the next day they worked in their 'clinic', the tent they had pitched by the side of the truck. They reassessed children that Jonathan had seen and been concerned about, checked the results of his treatment and saw new patients. Gena ably removed a long shard of wood embedded in a man's arm and drained the infection which had gathered around it. The man didn't seem to mind the procedure; he seemed to be watching Gena with fascination.

Richard gave a short laugh when he had gone. 'It seems we shall be able to use you as an anaesthetic,' he said to her.

She looked up at him in mock dismay. 'Is my conversation that boring?' she asked, and was rewarded again with his quick laugh.

And her spirits rose even further through the day as, for the first time, they worked comfortably together. Richard seemed positively companionable and good-humoured, and best of all he seemed to trust her to do the job.

When, next morning, it was time to leave, she was sorry. She had spent a pleasant evening by the fire endeavouring, amid shouts of laughter, to learn some of the villagers' language, and she felt she had made new friends. Richard had been as relaxed as she had ever seen him, sitting across from her at the fire, often watching her, and, as often as not, smiling.

He drove the truck. 'I must endeavour to redeem myself,' he explained.

Gena laughed. 'Oh, but you drove over the hardest bits,' she offered.

'Well, that is generous of you,' he replied, and Gena thought to herself that she could actually come to like this man.

And at the end of the day they agreed that he had redeemed himself. Not once was the truck in any real difficulty as they wound their way through the hills, and Gena watched in some admiration at the skill and judgement he showed in guiding it over a track that only faith told her existed at all. She found herself watching his hands, moving from wheel to gearstick and back, with pleasure. She noticed again how strong and dextrous and beautifully shaped they were.

Finally they stopped for the night. There was only a short stretch of road ahead before they reached their next village, but it was particularly difficult, Richard explained, and he didn't want to get stuck there with darkness falling. They would complete their journey in the morning.

Gena once more washed herself beneath the stars, and set about cooking their dinner. She had been thinking up a new recipe to try while they were driving along, and produced a surprisingly good dish from their meagre ingredients. They argued a little about its name.

'Beans Nuba,' suggested Richard.

'No, no,' cried Gena, 'it has to have a French name. This is *haute cuisine!*'

'I beg your pardon,' he said with great gravity, then brightened and offered *Haricots des Hills*, the 'H's silent.

'Wonderful!' she said, laughing. 'We could produce a cookbook. I'll supply the recipes——'

'And I'll eat them,' he finished.

'No, you supply the names. *The Sudan Cookbook*.' Gena paused a while, then said in a different tone, 'Actually it sounds like a sick joke, doesn't it?'

He looked up at her and made a wry face. 'Yes,' he said gently, 'it does a little.'

And, that night, Gena crawled over next to Richard as soon as she heard the hyenas' cry, and hardly felt embarrassed at all. He had been so friendly that day. Just the outline of him sleeping beside her was comforting. It was large and solid.

Even so, she trembled when the cries came closer. He seemed to know it straight away, though. And tonight, without a word, he put his arm around her, pressed one of her ears to his chest, and covered the other gently with his hand.

Gena sat on a rock and bit at a ragged part of her nail. It was daylight, but sunrise had not long gone. Richard had discovered a problem with the truck and was fixing it. Gena was thinking.

She was thinking specifically about the riddle that was Richard Maddison. A man who could be grim, unfriendly and unpleasant on the one hand, and do what he had done last night on the other.

She felt a flush spread over her face as she remembered how he had held her like a frightened child, and how, after her initial surprise had receded and her pulse had slowed, she had lain against his comforting warmth in the circle of his arm and gone to sleep.

She realised today that she felt differently towards him—more warmly, more gently. Whatever his reason for his previous coldness, he was not cold now. He had shown that he could be caring and kind, and that he had a very strong protective urge. It was something Gena particularly admired in a man—that desire to protect and nurture. Not all men had it, even doctors. And she reflected that she couldn't really care for a man who didn't. Perhaps they could come to be friends after all.

An hour later Gena was seeing why Richard had not wanted to press on the night before. Part of the track had collapsed beneath their wheel and the truck rested on its axles with two wheels deep in a gutter. If they could dig the hard earth under the axle out, the wheels would make contact in the gutter, and they could drive out, but getting underneath to do it was the difficulty.

'Give me the shovel, I can get in there,' said Gena.

'Mm. You're probably small enough, but you'll never dig into that ground,' said Richard.

She raised an eyebrow. 'Like hell I won't!' she said firmly, and took the shovel from his hands.

But he wasn't happy about it. 'Wait a minute,' he said. 'I don't want you under there. If you do budge it, it could settle on you.'

'If I leave my arm in the road, I deserve to have it crushed,' said Gena reasonably.

'None the less,' said Richard, 'I'd prefer you didn't have it crushed.'

'Well, I won't leave it in the road, then,' and with that she ended the argument by crawling in under the truck.

It was hard work, but not impossible, and after ten minutes or so Richard called to her, 'That'll do,' and she crawled out, dusty and sweating.

Richard looked at her and smiled, then started to climb into the cabin.

Gena looked down at herself. 'What are you grinning at?' she demanded.

He met her eyes, still smiling. 'Quite useful, really, aren't you?' he said.

'Of course I am!' she replied indignantly, as she scrambled into the truck. 'Whatever you may have thought at first.' Her blue eyes met his steadily.

'*Touché*,' he said with a rueful grin, and added, 'I should make you a formal apology, shouldn't I?'

'Yes,' she said simply.

'But you see,' he said, almost to himself, 'I'd never met a phenomenon like Gena Lamb.'

They visited three villages that day, and saw people who had not been contacted for quite some time. It was lucky for them in a way that they were so isolated. The measles hadn't reached them, and they were surprisingly healthy.

'These are some of the lucky ones of the Sudan,' Richard told her. 'The land in these valleys is fertile, and it allows them to grow enough for their needs. The water is good—no bilharzia.' He paused. 'It's one of the things that makes the work here so interesting—the regional variation. The major problems here are malaria, sleeping sickness, accidents. You'll see some burns from fires, and some septic wounds. One of the most useful things we can do up here is immunise against tetanus.'

And immunise they did, though many of the people seemed doubtful at first, and some of them downright afraid. Richard explained to them carefully, in their language, the purpose of the injection, in terms they would understand.

Gena did most of the injecting. Many of her patients were still clearly doubtful, but she spoke to them calmly in the Atema words that she knew, and seemed to inspire trust in them. Richard, seeing it, left her to do the job her own way.

At the end of the day, they stopped for the night on the outskirts of the last village.

'I'll sleep in the village tonight,' said Richard, 'if you'd like the tent to yourself.'

Gena glanced up quickly from their cooking fire

and swept her eyes with alarm over the lonely spot. 'No, thanks!' she said with feeling.

He smiled and put out an arm to give her a brief hug. 'It seems I'm useful too,' he said, grinning down at her blushing face.

But there were no hyenas that night, or Gena didn't hear them, and she awoke with a feeling of pleasant anticipation of the day ahead. She lay there for a while contentedly, wondering at how happy she felt. Perhaps this was the sort of thing she was really meant to do. She realised that she hadn't thought of Peter for days, and even now thinking of him failed to produce the feeling of grief and loss that had been there only days ago. Perhaps healing others also healed the self. Or perhaps it was just the joy of being in the bush, listening to the birds calling, lying in the peace of the silent night, sitting under the burning stars with a pleasant companion. And she realised that she was definitely coming to regard Richard as a pleasant companion and to enjoy his company. They had both been wrong about one another, but they were putting it behind them.

Late that day they came to a place of unparalleled beauty. Set among sheer red cliffs lay a still clear pool whose water glinted in the late afternoon sunlight.

Gena exclaimed, and Richard steered the truck as close to the edge of the rock-pool as he could.

'It's formed from a spring,' he told her. 'Quite cold.'

'Can we swim in it?' she asked excitedly, and he nodded readily. Gena needed no second bidding. It was the first large body of water she'd seen in the Sudan, and infinitely inviting. 'I haven't got anything to swim in,' she said.

'I shall avert my eyes,' said Richard gravely, and suited the action to the words, turning his back on her.

In two minutes she was in the water, and gasping. 'You weren't joking about the cold!' she called, and turned to see Richard peeling his own clothes off.

She dived down under the surface and revelled in the feeling of the cold water in her hair and on her hot face. When she resurfaced, Richard was a little way from her, standing in waist-deep water and washing the dust off his neck and arms.

He was quite beautiful, she suddenly thought— big, muscular, and perfectly proportioned. She felt a strange sensation gather in her. Odd, she thought to herself as she turned away, she had never felt so moved by masculine beauty before. Perhaps it was the place. Exposed to the wild loveliness of Africa, perhaps she'd become more sensitive to natural beauty in all its forms.

The pool shallowed on the far side and she stood not quite waist-deep there with her back to Richard, enjoying the feeling of the sun on her now cool body. She squeezed the water out of her hair and it lay, golden and streaming, on the nape of her neck. She stood there for a while, as still as a statue, letting the sun sink into her, in order to enjoy the cool again.

At last she sank back into the water, and turned to see Richard leaning back against a rock, regarding her.

'It's lovely,' she said, to cover her sudden awkwardness.

'Mmm.' His reply was the barest murmur.

Later, in clean clothes, they squatted on rocks and washed the dust out of the things they had worn. They would certainly not take long to dry in this climate. Richard also filled up the water tanks and put water in the radiator.

They were silent with one another for the rest of the afternoon. They seemed lost in a sort of dreamy languor as they headed for the highest point, and the turning point, of their trek.

'There's only one more tribe,' said Richard later as they camped on the hilltop. 'We didn't really need to come up this far.' He paused. 'I wanted you to see the view from here in the morning.'

Gena met his eyes. 'Thank you,' she said, smiling.

'There may be one disadvantage to being here,' he admitted. 'You may hear more noises in the night.'

'Oh,' she said. 'Oh, well, I'm used to them now. They can't get into the tent, after all.'

'Not unless they've learned to undo knots since I was here last,' he agreed.

She looked at him balefully. 'I wish you hadn't said that!'

The night was completely still when they crawled into their sleeping-bags, and the only noises they could hear were the small sounds of darkness—the chirruping insects and far-off calls of night-time birds. Without wind, it was sultry, and the air seemed to hang heavily on them.

Despite the peace of the place, Gena found she didn't drop into an exhausted sleep as she had the other nights. She unzipped her sleeping-bag and threw it off her, thinking the heat was keeping her awake, but still she lay there watching the sky through the tent fly.

Richard rolled over on to his back. He lay on top of his sleeping-bag, not in it.

'Can't sleep?' His deep voice came from his side of the tent.

'No. Somehow I don't feel tired tonight.'

'It's hotter than it has been,' he observed.

'Mm. I'd like another swim in that pool.' And suddenly Gena was remembering it—sunshine dancing on clear cold water, the feel of it on her hot body, and the sight of Richard, beautiful, strong, brown, natural. Unaccountably, her heart began to hammer and a new heat stole through her. She rolled over and pulled the sleeping-bag off her altogether. In doing so, she touched Richard's outflung arm, and felt as though a bolt of electricity had passed through her.

She lay on her side, quite still, breathing quickly, unable or unwilling to give this feeling a name. And then she felt his hand on hers and moving slowly

with a caressing motion up her bare arm. Slowly she
felt his fingers run along the softness of her upper
arm and over the smooth curve of her shoulder. She
held her breath, unable to think what it meant. His
hand seemed to tremble suddenly on her shoulder,
and in a moment it was withdrawn.

His voice seemed strangely hoarse as he said,
'Goodnight,' and rolled away from her.

It had been a friendly gesture, but it left no doubt
in Gena's mind as to what her own feelings had
meant. She had to admit that she was strongly
attracted to this man, and further, that the emotion
she had experienced was far more violent than any
of its kind she had felt before.

As far as physical passion went, Gena acknowledged that she was still a child, quite unawakened.
Had been a child, she corrected mentally. For now
she began to know what she hadn't known before.
Her intellect sent her warnings not to confuse this
with love. This was a physical attraction, she told
herself, completely different from what she had felt
for Peter. That had been mental. And then she was
suddenly seized with doubt that what she had felt
for Peter had been anything more than friendship.
Should she not have felt some of this delicious,
disturbing feeling?

She suddenly seemed to see Peter more clearly
than she ever had before—as an amicable, charming
boy, clever and likeable, but a boy none the less,
and not to be compared with the exciting, powerful,
dangerous man beside her.

Dangerous, she mused. Yes, it was true. For he was dangerous now in a new way. He had the power to disturb her thoughts and stir her feelings, perhaps even to affect her behaviour. No, that mustn't be. She must deal with these new feelings sensibly. They were only natural—he was a very attractive man. But she mustn't place too much importance on them. She must continue to be his colleague, and, hopefully, his friend, and keep all other feelings under control.

'You're not afraid of those cats?' he asked her suddenly, and added drily, 'Of being eaten?'

Gena gave a short laugh. 'Maybe I am. I—I don't know. Maybe it's just hot.' She didn't want to lie close to Richard Maddison tonight.

'Don't be,' he said quietly. 'I wouldn't let anything hurt you.'

In the morning Gena awoke to the odd experience of being watched while she slept. She was still at Richard's side and he was propped up on his arm, his eyes on her face. It made her blush.

'I've counted your arms and legs,' he said wryly. 'You only came with two apiece, didn't you?'

A laugh burst from her that dispelled all her shyness.

'We'll start back towards Kosti this afternoon,' he told her, adding, 'That means more sand.'

It certainly did! After affectionate farewells from the remaining tribe, whom they vaccinated against the measles epidemic which hadn't reached them yet, they crawled once again out of the hills, to the north-east this time. From the last hill, Gena saw the red-brown sandy plain stretch out before them.

But somehow the prospect was not at all daunting. They had learned to rely on one another, and their now easy companionship buoyed Gena up. They laughed together as they dug the Land Rover out of the first sand-drift and then the second. Richard curled his lip at her after she had insisted she could drive better and had bogged them in their third, which made her laugh more.

When they reached the first of their stopping places on the dry plain, however, their laughter faded. These people were very different from the tribes of the Nuba hills. Living on the edge of starvation, in an ever-growing desert, they were a miserable people, afflicted by all the diseases that such hardships brought. The children were pathetic scarecrows, with grotesquely swollen bellies, who sat so forlornly still it was as though they already anticipated the death that would probably soon overtake them.

'They've had no relief for a month,' said Richard grimly when he rejoined her after talking to the men.

'What can we do?' she asked, and her voice was unsteady.

He looked at her a moment, but Gena turned away to hide the unshed tears.

'Go straight back to Udari,' he said. 'I'll get on

the radio there and see what I can organise. These people need food before medicine.'

And so it was that they churned through the miles of sand between this desolate spot and their own small oasis. The laughter was gone, but there dwelt a gentleness between them that came of sharing pain.

And on the way home they shared also a little of their histories, in the way of people becoming friends. Richard was introduced to Gena's parents, and became acquainted with the town she had grown up in. She learned that Richard's father had been a country vet. He had no doubt that it had been the basis for his interest in medicine, but his concern was with people, not animals. He had always known he would be a doctor.

'You must have known early, too,' he remarked.

'Oh, no!' she cried. 'I was going to be a ballerina. And a kindergarten teacher, and a dog-breeder, and an astronaut.'

He laughed out loud, then turned to look at her. 'Really?' he asked. 'Deep down?'

Gena smiled. 'Well, maybe not,' she conceded. 'Maybe, deep down, it was medicine.'

Richard's grey eyes smiled back at her. 'Good thing,' he said.

But the compliment escaped her. She was still dealing with the feelings engendered by those smiling eyes.

When they finally drove through the gates of the hospital, Gena reflected how much her feelings had changed about the man who sat at her side, and suspected that his had too. Perhaps she had proven herself sufficiently, or perhaps she had only imagined his old dislike.

CHAPTER EIGHT

THE change in their relationship was readily apparent to their colleagues. Jonathan remarked on it first, in his usual style.

'You two seem to have become awfully chummy,' he said. 'Have you been taken off the list of unsuitables?'

'I think it was my way with a shovel,' said Gena.

Jonathan laughed. 'Good heavens! You don't mean to say he had you digging the truck out? I always manage to be so useless at it that he does it himself.'

'I enjoyed the exercise,' she said, and Jonathan shook his head.

'Strange girl,' he observed. 'Must be the excessive heat in your homeland.'

Matron and Angus both welcomed the change. They had come to like Gena in the short time they had known her, and wanted her to be happy here. And neither had any doubts as to her worth. Heather demanded a moment-by-moment account of the trip, and still seemed vaguely dissatisfied at the end of it. Perhaps she felt that no newcomer could be as much use to Richard as she and Pauline. She seemed more restless and fidgety than before they had gone away, or perhaps Gena had become used to Richard's calm repose.

Of all the staff at the hospital, only Pauline remained aloof from Gena, and Gena now had the additional unpleasant sensation of being watched by her. Sitting on the veranda in the evening quietly discussing the events of the day with Angus or Richard, she would have this presentiment and look up to find the girl's gaze upon her, brooding and watchful. She was certainly an unusual woman, Gena thought.

But she soon forgot Pauline completely when, a few days later, there occurred an incident which cast a spanner into the works of their new-found friendship.

Richard had asked her to send off some blood tests to Khartoum on a patient in the hospital. Gena had taken the blood and placed the tubes in a box of other things which were going to the hospital there. But when Richard radioed the next afternoon for the important results, the specimens hadn't been received.

Gena was in the hospital laboratory when Richard approached her, a frown on his face. He came straight to the point. 'Gena, I know you have a lot to do here, but those blood tests were important. I was expecting to have the results today.'

She looked at him blankly for a moment, then frowned. 'You should have them today. They went yesterday morning.'

He looked at her steadily for a moment. 'I've radioed the hospital, and they weren't received.'

'Oh, no!' exclaimed Gena. 'I wonder where they are, then.'

'You're saying you sent them?' he asked, frowning again.

'Of course I did,' she replied. 'I don't just ignore your requests. I put them in the box with the other things, and told Angus they were ready.'

There was a longer silence as the man regarded the girl measuringly. 'They received the other things, but not the blood.'

'But that's ridiculous!' she burst out. 'They can't have got one thing and not the other. They were together in the box.'

Richard sat down on the laboratory stool and sighed. 'Gena, if you forget something, or make a mistake, for God's sake don't lie to me. That destroys our professional relationship, as no mistake ever could.'

Gena flushed red to the roots of her hair, an occurrence owing as much to a sudden mounting anger as to any other emotion. 'You're really accusing me of lying,' she said indignantly.

'It's a little difficult to do anything else,' he said, his voice growing hard. 'Angus picked the box up from here, taped it up without removing anything and put it on the plane. Yet the blood samples weren't received.'

'That doesn't make sense,' she said flatly. 'The lab at the hospital must have lost them.'

Richard slowly shook his head, his face serious.

ARE YOU A FAN
OF MILLS & BOON
MEDICAL ROMANCES?

IF YOU are a regular United Kingdom buyer of Mills & Boon Medical Romances you might like to tell us your opinion of the books we publish to help us in publishing the books *you* like.

Mills & Boon have a Reader Panel of Medical Romance readers. Each person on the panel receives a questionnaire every third month asking her for *her* opinion of the past twelve Medical Romances. All people who send in their replies have a chance of winning a FREE year's supply of Medical Romances.

If YOU would like to be considered for inclusion on the Panel please give us details about yourself below. We can't guarantee that everyone will be on the panel but first come will be first considered. All postage will be free. Younger readers are particularly welcome.

Year of birth .... Month ....

Age at completion of full-time education ....

Single ☐ Married ☐ Widowed ☐ Divorced ☐

If any children at home, their ages please ....

Your name (print please) ....

Address ....

....

.... Postcode ....

THANK YOU! PLEASE TEAR OUT AND POST
NO STAMP NEEDED IN THE U.K.

DR1190/RD

2 1

He didn't believe she had sent them. Gena suddenly knew a desperate need to convince him.

'OK,' she cried, 'go and ask the patient whether I took the blood. She'll remember. I took the blood. I filled a blue tube and a pink tube, then I put them in a plastic bag, labelled. I put the bag in the box——'

'Are you sure you did that?' he interrupted. 'All right, I accept that you took the blood and packaged it. But are you sure you put it in the box? You didn't leave it on a bench anywhere?' His eyes searched the room.

'No.' Gena was adamant. 'No, no, no! I put it in the box. Richard, I'm certain. Do you really think I would lie to you?'

The hurt on her face was matched now by something almost the same on his own.

'I didn't think you would, no,' he replied softly. After a time spent contemplating nothing in particular, he sighed again. 'OK, let's forget it, Gena. Let's start again. Take some more blood and we'll send it in the morning.'

'But, Richard,' she protested, 'where did it go?' then wished she hadn't asked. There was no answer to the question.

The next parcel of blood was received and processed, but there was no such satisfactory ending to Gena's enquiries on the subject. No one had taken the blood tubes out of the box. No one had been near the box. Angus, though sympathetic, was sure he had simply taped it up. They would never know.

It cast a shadow over her relationship with Richard. She felt he was more distant with her, and put this down to his belief that she had lied. For her part, she was more than a little angry with him for believing it.

Jonathan had gone back towards Kosti, which, she told herself, was another reason she was feeling a little disconsolate. She was missing his company. She was very glad when he returned.

'So the honeymoon's over, is it?' he asked when he saw the change in the situation. 'I knew you'd come to your senses.'

Gena grimaced. 'More a case of my being back on the unsuitable list, I'm afraid.'

'Inevitable, my dear girl. That's our fearless leader for you—excellent doctor, but an innate mistrust of women.'

'Do you think that's true?' Gena asked.

'Stands to reason,' said Jonathan flatly. 'Late thirties, unmarried, a confirmed misogynist.'

'I wondered about that.'

Jonathan gave her an appraising look. 'You're not—er——'

Gena returned his look sternly. 'Not what?' she said repressively.

'No, of course not,' he said quickly. 'Forget I mentioned it. And let's talk about more pleasant things than the irascible Richard Maddison. Let's talk about stealing the truck and driving to Khartoum and dancing the night away in a nightclub.'

Gena laughed. 'That would make us popular!'

'Ah, it would be pleasant, though, you must admit.' Dreamily, he seized her and spun her round the sitting-room floor in a slow dance, singing, 'You made me love you. . .'

He sang quite well, Gena thought, and danced very well, with a light step and good rhythm. She was actually enjoying herself for the first time in some days when Richard came in to ask Jonathan whether the relief truck had got to the camp near Kosti.

It had got there. The people had clustered around the truck in their hundreds as the sacks of grain were unloaded, desperately afraid that their children would be the ones to miss out, willing to do anything to hold on to those fragile threads of life a little longer, till the gods should stop punishing their people and send more rains.

Jonathan described the arrangements they had made for storing and guarding the grain, and the system of rationing. Richard grunted his satisfaction with the plan.

'It should last them a month,' said Jonathan. 'If there's no rain in that time. . .' He shook his head.

Within a few days of Jonathan's return, Gena had cheered up markedly. He entertained her with stories of the blunders he had made, and the missing blood tubes began to seem a little thing. Still a vexatious thing, because she was still sure she had put them in the box, but a little vexatious thing.

She and Jonathan consulted with one another about patients, whiled away evenings chatting on the veranda, and once drove to the other side of Udari to an odd little roadside stop at an oasis. There they sat in the shade of the one tree and drank the sweet tea that was taken several times a day all over the Sudan.

'That way lies Khartoum,' pronounced Jonathan, sweeping his arm out over the sandy plain.

'What's it like?' asked Gena. 'All I saw was the rooftops from the plane, and the airport.'

He mused a while. 'Fascinating—dirty, crowded, noisy. But it has a magic at night, a mystery. You never know what might happen in its opium dens and alleyways.'

He had spoken with drama, and she laughed. 'Really?'

'Oh, yes,' he said. 'You'd better not go there, little Gena. You're so beautiful, you might get sold into white slavery.'

She laughed again, but blushed as well. 'That's an awfully nice thing to say.'

'Well, I'm an awfully nice chap,' he said with a grin. 'A trifle unreliable, but awfully nice.'

'I believe you are,' said Gena seriously. 'And I'm glad you're here.'

She was. She liked him, and his company was very pleasant, but even so she didn't cheer up completely until the day when Richard took her to see some patients in the town and gave every appearance of having forgotten all about the blood tests. They walked back at dusk, chatting happily about what they had seen and what they ought to do.

'You learn quickly,' Richard told her. 'One of the hardest lessons for a doctor from a civilised country is what can be done here, and what can't. Sometimes you seem to know it instinctively.'

Gena flushed with pleasure at the compliment. 'Don't forget I've worked with Australians who in many ways live similar lives to these people.'

'The Aboriginals?'

She nodded.

By the time they gained the residence, Gena felt that the episode of the blood tests had been thrust firmly into the background. They were friends and colleagues again, and she wondered if that had been his aim in taking her to the town. He certainly didn't need her medical opinion, she reflected. They were laughing together as they mounted the residence steps.

Richard suggested a gin and tonic, which sounded like a good idea to Gena, and she arranged herself comfortably in one of the veranda chairs while he went to get it. A movement caught her eye at the other end of the veranda as she leant her head back against the chair, and she realised suddenly that Pauline had been standing there. She was about to call to the girl to join them in a drink, when the silent form slipped away through the sitting-room doors.

Odd, mused Gena. She was a very odd woman. Dedicated to her job, knowledgeable and thorough, she was an excellent nurse. But she was almost totally cut off from the others. Not even Matron

seemed close to her, though their working relationship seemed very good. And she was so often to be
seen as Gena had seen her just now—standing in
the shadows, seemingly watching them with her
large dark eyes burning with something unguessable.

Jonathan said it was religious fervour, and main-
tained that she was slightly mad. Gudwe said she
was a witch.

'You stay way,' he had told Gena. 'She make
trouble, you come see me—I give you magic for her.
Got plenty magic—magic for bad people, magic for
love, magic for babies.' He'd looked from Gena to
Jonathan and back in a way the meaning of which
couldn't be escaped, grinning broadly.

Jonathan had grinned back, while Gena had
choked into her gin and tonic.

'Thank you, Gudwe,' Jonathan had said. 'I'll let
you know when I need some of that magic!'

Gudwe had slapped him on the shoulder, pleased
that a white man was showing some sense at last.

The following day dawned as peaceably as any other.
The first Gena knew of the incident which would
plunge her into so much trouble and misery was
when she was called urgently to the children's ward
by a young native nurse who had clearly been
running.

Gena ran herself, all sorts of dire imaginings
flashing through her mind. When she got there, the
truth was no less dramatic. Richard was pumping
oxygen into a child while Matron was rhythmically

depressing his little chest with her hand. It was a cardiac arrest.

'Get a line into his vein,' ordered Richard.

Gena did it, rapidly.

'Give him the narcan,' he said, and one of the native sisters handed it to her, the clear liquid in a syringe whose function was to reverse the effects of an overdose of narcotics. Gena squirted it in, and asked for some sterile saline to flush it through the veins with.

'Get the Life Pak connected,' said Richard, his voice remaining even and calm.

Gena attached the small brown body to the machine, called a Life Pak, which showed on a screen the patient's heart rhythm and which could be used to give electric shocks if that rhythm was not compatible with life.

In the case of this child, it was not. The machine showed a flat line instead of the usual tracing with regular peaks and bumps. He was in total cardiac standstill.

Gena asked for adrenalin, and it was brought in a syringe. The injection of adrenalin might get the child's heart going without having to resort to shocks. She looked at Richard, and, holding the syringe, raised her eyebrows in a question.

He nodded briefly.

She squirted half the adrenalin out on to the floor. He was a child and required a child's dose, even of this. The rest she injected into the line in his vein. Then she watched the screen.

Almost at once the straight line leapt into life, at first in disorganised bumps and wriggles, then into a halting semblance of normal form and finally into a beautiful even series of upstrokes, downstrokes and curves that signified a return to normal.

Gena let a breath out. 'Sinus rhythm,' she said.

And, as though he'd been informed of this, the small patient began to moan and move and push the oxygen mask away.

'Good output,' said Richard, his fingers on the tiny pulse.

Matron endeavoured to comfort the child, telling him over and over that he was all right now, it was all over, to be a good boy and breathe the nice oxygen; and he listened to her soothing firm voice and breathed away, his eyes big above the mask.

'What happened?' asked Gena. The child had a broken leg; there was no reason for his heart to stop.

And Richard reached over for the child's chart, flipped over the pages to the one where orders for medication were written and wordlessly held it out to her. There, above her own signature, written clearly in the same pen was the order: 'Pethidine 200 milligrams, every six hours, by mouth.'

Gena gasped. The skin on her face prickled, and her heart thumped in her chest. She hadn't ordered this. The child was four years old. The dose was twenty milligrams. She hadn't ordered two hundred.

She looked at Richard and shook her head, speechless. He looked back at her, a sort of pain in his face. 'I didn't order this!' she cried at last, and saw his face empty itself of expression. 'Two hundred!' she continued. 'It's a fatal overdose! I ordered twenty.'

And suddenly she realised how it sounded. First the blood tubes, and now this. And there was two hundred written in neat round figures beneath her name. It was there. It had been ordered. What was she saying? That someone had added an extra nought for her?

Gena felt a chill creep over her entire body. For she realised that she was saying exactly that. She had thought carefully about the dose of painkiller to give this child. She had written it out carefully, as always. She remembered writing it. She remembered writing twenty in clear figures. She looked again at the order. The figures were evenly spaced, but there was not as much room as there would normally be between the last, almost fatal nought, and the following word.

Someone had altered it—carefully and well, with the same kind of black pen.

Gena's brain span as it groped for an explanation. Who? Why? It was fantastic, incredible. And her mind steadied itself on the word 'incredible'. That was what it was. And no one would believe it. Who would alter a drug dose to kill an innocent four-year-old child? What possible reason could anyone have for doing so? No one was going to believe her, least of all Richard. Gena felt the tears beginning to well in her eyes.

'There's no more for you to do here,' said Richard. 'Why don't you go back to the residence?' His voice was devoid of expression.

She went.

In her room, Gena flung herself down on her bed and wept the bitterest tears of her life. A child had almost died, and she was to be blamed. And she hadn't been responsible. Someone, somewhere in the hospital, for some reason that was impossible to guess, had tried to kill the child. Somewhere in the hospital was a mind evil and deranged enough to kill, perhaps for sport.

For it was the only explanation that occurred to her. So fantastic an explanation was it that Gena examined for a moment the possibility that she *had* written two hundred milligrams. But it wasn't so! She remembered writing it. Could one remember wrongly? Only if one were mad, she concluded, and she wasn't mad.

And suddenly Pauline's face swam into her mind. The association with madness, no doubt. But she shook her head clear of the irrelevant vision. There was no way that Pauline could have had any hand in it. She was dedicated and religious. Gena could not believe her oddness included a disposition to murder children.

An hour later, Richard came to see her, and, if Gena had thought she had already plumbed the depths of misery, she realised when he had gone again that she was wrong. He had not attacked her or denounced her, or even raised his voice. He had simply said that he couldn't understand how she could have made such a mistake. He had blamed the sister too, and had said she should have known enough to query the excessive order.

Gena suddenly felt that if she accepted the blame, everything would be easier. Richard would be disappointed and would cease to trust her. He might even, under his judicious calm, be angry. But it was an anger not to be compared to that which he would show her if she denied responsibility. Miserably, she contemplated the options.

She could not do it. For a start, it let the real culprit go unsuspected. And who knew? It might happen again.

She took a deep breath and prepared to answer him. 'Richard,' she started, 'I know that you have doubts about me because of the blood tests. And I know also that it sounds crazy for me to say that I didn't write that order the way it was, because if that's true, then someone must have changed it, and who would do that, and why. . .?' Her voice trailed away miserably for a moment, and Richard answered, his face tight.

'Exactly,' was all he said.

Gena gathered her courage. 'So what I'm saying to you is that I believe I remember writing it, and I believe I wrote twenty. Now, maybe I'm wrong. Maybe I'm crazy. . .' The tears welled up again in her eyes and she brushed them away. 'But I have to say it, because if I'm not crazy, someone else in this hospital is.'

There was a long silence, then Richard spoke with a grimness that seemed to twist something inside her. 'Very well,' he said, 'I accept the possibility that one can do one thing while thinking one has done something else. I don't accept the possibility that anyone in this hospital could have purposely altered that drug order.' And the anger that she had dreaded seemed to kindle in him suddenly. 'You realise that you're accusing one of your colleagues of attempted murder?' he blazed.

A sob escaped her, in reply.

He seemed to make an effort to control himself, but Gena could see the anger plainly now. His face was white, his jaw taut. He went on, 'It mustn't happen again. Twice now—that's enough. This time it could have meant a child's life.' He stood up and looked at her for a long moment before he spoke again. 'Keep your mind on the job. No more mistakes.' He turned and strode away.

The days that followed had the quality of a nightmare for Gena. Angus and Jonathan were kind, but their sympathy didn't seem to help. Jonathan endeavoured to cheer her by every means he could think of, but that didn't help either.

Gena had expected to encounter more than the usual aloofness from Pauline, and had somehow feared it, but no change in the sister's attitude could be discerned. It was Heather's reaction, in the event, that upset her most. Her frequent references to the matter were made in a sympathetic vein. Anyone could have done it, she declared. But it made Gena grit her teeth. For she hadn't done it; and just occasionally Gena wondered whether there wasn't just a little touch of triumph. Thank God the girl seemed less restless now and was no longer driving Gena insane by kicking her chair at mealtimes. It was enough to have Gudwe nagging at her for picking at her food!

The fact remained that no one doubted that she had ordered that fatal dose, and though there were times when Gena almost believed she must have, a small stubborn part of herself still cried, You're innocent. And there's danger here.

Richard treated her with a polite formality that made her utterly miserable. She began to feel she would prefer him angry. And what confounded her completely was that she could still feel his attraction, despite his reserve. For every now and again his eyes would meet with hers and she would feel that surge of exciting warmth again; or she would see him at his work, tender with his patients, his voice deep and gentle, his hands strong and sure.

As the days went on and he remained distantly civil, she was assailed by an increasing sense of loss. She realised that, as brief as it had been, their friendship had been very pleasant to her. Now it was gone forever. With pain she remembered scenes from their patrol to the mountains—Richard's hands on the wheel of the truck, his quiet laugh when she said something to amuse him, the comfort of his arm when she was frightened, the set of his broad shoulders, a smile in his grey eyes, looking warmly at her as they never did now.

He was a good man, and a good doctor, and would have been a good friend. But he thought she had let herself be distracted in her job and had not had the courage to admit her mistake. He thought she was prepared to implicate her colleagues to save herself.

Miserably, Gena had to admit to herself that he had every right to withdraw his friendship.

And then that small stubborn voice would arise in her again, and it was an angry voice. He could have listened to you. He could have trusted you. He could at least have considered the possibility that you were telling the truth.

She turned more and more to Jonathan. Angus was a nice man, but he was Richard's friend, and it made Gena feel uncomfortable that she might be engendering divided loyalties. And Jonathan was of her own generation, though a few years older. He became the brother she'd never had, and she his little sister.

Each of them knew instinctively that it would never be more, and they didn't have to talk about it. It made their relationship superbly comfortable.

Sometimes on their time off they walked together for miles across the open country, Jonathan with a rifle carelessly slung across his back just in case.

'Can you actually use that thing?' she asked.

'God, no. I shall probably shoot myself.'

She giggled. 'As long as you don't shoot me!'

'I won't do that,' he said emphatically. 'That would be ungallant, and I'm never ungallant.'

'Except maybe where Pauline and Heather are concerned?' she suggested.

'I've never called her the Praying Mantis to her face,' he pointed out sweetly. 'And I think I'm very gallant with Heather. I've listened to her disordered ravings for almost a year now and I've never once told her to put a sock in it.'

'Yes, that's very commendable, of course,' replied Gena solemnly.

'It is.' He grinned. 'You must admit that Africa attracts some strange people. Richard. . . Pauline . . . Heather.'

'Heather? I don't think she's strange,' said Gena.

'Don't you?' Jonathan frowned for a moment. 'She says some odd things at times. She almost seems to believe in the native stuff—magic and all that. And the rumour is that she followed Richard out here. Now you won't tell me that isn't strange behaviour.'

Gena laughed, despite herself. 'I think I understand, though,' she said tentatively, 'why a nurse might be inspired to follow his lead.'

Jonathan groaned. 'Now you *are* making me worried!'

When they crossed the compound that evening after their walk, Richard was there, and disapproving.

'You're back far too late,' he said to Jonathan.

'You should know better than to wander round with her in the dusk out there.'

'I can protect her,' answered Jonathan shortly, and the two men faced each other silently for a moment.

Then Richard gave a little grunt, which might have been derision, and turned on his heel.

'That's the attitude I can't stand,' said Jonathan. 'The attitude that he's the only one capable of looking after things.'

Gena sympathised, and didn't tell him that she herself had been feeling anxious in the gathering gloom. She was fond of Jonathan, but he didn't inspire the same trust as Richard Maddison, for all his faults.

The knowledge did nothing to make her feel better. And the result of the conflict in her was that she began to think of leaving. It seemed somehow pointless to stay here now. She was miserable, and despite the best efforts of the others, and her friendship with Jonathan, she often felt as alone as Pauline.

Then in the space of a day or two, personal feelings became irrelevant and thoughts of leaving Udari impossible.

CHAPTER NINE

THE first intimation of the horror to come was only a thin trickle of patients at the hospital clinic with dry coughs and aching muscles. They were symptoms seen with many viral infections and only worrying in this instance in that they seemed to be making the patients sicker than usual. In a few days, however, it began to be evident that this was a virus with a difference, and that it was present in epidemic proportions.

It was clearly an influenza. It started with perhaps a sniffle or a sore throat, and quickly went on to prostrate its victims with a high fever, a terrible hacking cough and pains all over the body. It left them in some cases too weak to get out of their beds.

And Richard Maddison, experienced in such epidemics, feared worse. 'The ordinary viral illness is bad enough for these people,' he said. 'Some of them, especially the old and the children, will die from that alone. But a certain percentage, and it could be high, will go on to get a pneumonia as well.'

They were sitting at the dining-room table, where Richard had called them. They needed to plan their response to the threat before them.

Richard sat at the head of the table, his good-looking face showing his worry. 'We'll have the hospital full and overflowing in a week,' he predicted. 'That means more work than we can handle with all of us here. And we won't have all of us here, because this hasn't originated in the town. It was brought to the town from out west. Some of us will have to go out and do what we can for the people there. That means you, initially, Angus, and if the situation's bad enough probably Jonathan too.'

He thought awhile. 'Angus, you'd better go into Khartoum today on the plane. We'll need a hell of a lot more of everything. If it's not available there, get on to Nairobi and have it sent by air. Wait for it.'

The older man nodded.

'Matron Potts, you know the procedure here already. We need to set up as many additional beds as we can, and get as much additional help from the town as we can. Not for face-to-face nursing, though. That can only be done by the staff we have. They have a reasonable chance of being immune to this.' He glanced at Pauline Hickey. 'Pauline, Matron will have her work cut out supervising the face-to-face nursing staff. The additional volunteers will have to be your responsibility. Use them as effectively as you can, and try not to place them at risk. Instruct them in how to cut down their risk of getting it. I know you'll do an excellent job.'

'Yes, Dr Maddison. Thank you,' she said eagerly, her large eyes shining.

He turned to Gena. 'You and I will have to

manage an overflowing hospital between the two of us a lot of the time. It won't be easy. We won't have time to eat or sleep. We'll have a dozen things to do at once. We'll be constantly tired.'

Gena thought he was warning her subtly, as he had before out loud, 'Keep your mind on the job. No more mistakes.' But she stuffed down her hurt and anger, and answered lightly, 'Sounds like internship all over again!'

She was rewarded with perhaps the first smile he had given her since the cardiac arrest, and was unprepared for the effect it had on her. It seemed at once to flood her with warmth and to make her feel like crying.

He only replied, 'That's right, Gena. A sense of humour is going to be pretty important.'

He hadn't been kidding, Gena reflected four days later, as she bent over the sink and splashed cold water on her face. It was six o'clock and she had fallen into bed at three. The only place where Richard had been out was in his estimate of the speed with which things would progress. Four days down the line and the hospital was already full.

The Africans were 'going down like ninepins' to it, to use an old phrase of her father's. Already, beds on the floor were occupied, and the sight of another makeshift ward being set up on the hospital veranda taught Gena that the worst hadn't hit them.

There were cases of pneumonia already, as well as those who were at risk of dying of dehydration, febrile convulsions or heart failure in the case of the elderly. The dispensary was piled with boxes full of precious fluids and medicines. A small army of volunteers laboured under Pauline's direction to try and keep up a supply of food and linen, and to keep the wards clean.

Already they were working harder than Gena had ever had to work before, Richard calmly and smoothly like a well-oiled machine, Jonathan in a sort of manic state.

'God,' he groaned on the evening of the fourth day. 'I didn't know I could work this hard!'

Richard, who had come to look at Jonathan's patient, looked as though he would like to agree. He bent down to listen to the child's chest.

'How are you doing, young Gena?' asked Jonathan, giving her a hug. 'Are you holding up all right?'

'Apart from my feet, I'm fine,' she said.

'I'll give them a long, sensuous massage when this is all over,' he promised.

She smiled.

Richard, looking up from the patient's side, wasn't smiling. 'You haven't replaced enough fluid,' he said briefly. 'He's still dehydrated. I can't see anything else.' He strode away, back to his own work.

'The workload doesn't seem to bother him, does it?' said Jonathan, staring after him. 'You know, I don't think he's one of us.'

'What?' asked Gena, beginning to grin for the first time in days.

'I think he's an android—you know, a robot. Maybe he and Heather have been sent together from outer space. She's not human either.'

'Oh, no,' laughed Gena, 'not Heather. She's human. Even her boundless energy has been taxed by this. I saw her flop into a chair last night as though she'd never get up again.'

'Oh. Well, he's not from earth, anyway. He's a sophisticated human-looking computer.'

Gena smiled wistfully to herself. I wonder if that's almost true, she thought. I wonder if he has ever cared for anyone? Maybe his friendliness in the hills was just an extension of his bedside manner, easy to switch off again when she displeased him. Why was he alone here? Was he capable of real feelings, for anyone except his patients? Perhaps, after all, the only thing he really cared about was medicine.

The suffering of the people was terrible.

On Friday, Angus's truck arrived back, driven by Gudwe, who had gone with him. It was bad among the Arabs. He brought with him a list of supplies that were needed, and a request for Jonathan.

On Saturday, a week after their meeting, Jonathan left for the Arab settlements in the west, and the veranda ward began to fill. They lay there, the patients, side by side on rush mats. Those with drips up had the plastic bottles attached to nails in the veranda wall. They had long ago run out of drip stands. Here and there an oxygen bottle bubbled away into the masks of the worst afflicted patients, but there weren't many of them available, not nearly enough.

Some patients tossed and moaned with their fevers, but most lay still, resigned to their suffering. It was terribly hot. The nurses sponged the worst afflicted with tepid water and helpers fanned them with rush fans while the water evaporated for maximum effect.

Matron did the drug round, with the stainless steel trolley, tirelessly drawing up antibiotics, giving drugs to treat the fever and the vomiting and the pain. Heather took temperatures, blood-pressures, pulses, and measured urine outputs. She calculated the total fluids in and out of the patients, so that Gena would know how much they would need in the next eight hours.

Pauline and Gena took blood samples, and Gena took them to the lab to look at there or to send on to Khartoum. If only they had some blood analysis machines right there! Decisions had to be made on the basis of the clinical state of the patient. Richard had been right: you had to back your judgement. There were no experts or technicians to rely on. There were difficult decisions to be made. Was this patient well enough to go home now, or should he stay longer? Was another sick enough to warrant admission? Another of their precious beds gone. Yet more work for them all. Was this woman's microscope slide clear because she had no bacteria in her lungs? Or had they got a sample of sputum that

wasn't good enough, mostly saliva? Gena would
have to do it again. More precious time.

'Had anything to eat today?' Richard asked Gena
as he passed her in the ward.

She frowned. 'I can't remember,' she said, and it
was true. One day was beginning to run into the
next. Sleep was snatched whenever it could be, and
day and night meant nothing. Richard didn't seem
to sleep at all.

'Go and get something,' he said.

'I just want to put this drip in,' she told him, but
he put a firm hand on her shoulder and drew her
away from the bed.

'And after that there'll be another one, and
another,' he said firmly. 'Go and get something now.
You seem to be tougher than I'd ever imagined,
Gena, but your strength's not inexhaustible.'

Is yours? Gena wondered, but didn't say it.

It seemed to be. He slept half as much as she and
coped with more cases. He continued to be gentle
and comforting with people in the searing heat and
the turmoil of the overflowing wards. As always, his
diagnoses were accurate and his treatment swift and
efficient. It was not always effective. Patients died,
and he found time to comfort the relatives, before
moving on to the next ones.

He was encouraging and patient with the staff. He
kept them going. The mere presence of his tall,
powerful frame in the ward, the sound of his voice
low and calm was as comforting to the overworked
nurses as the patients.

Watching him bending over a small patient, Gena was reminded of the night he had held her when the hyenas were calling and felt how nice it would be to be held in those strong arms now.

He seemed to sense her watching him, and looked up. Gena hastily attempted to erase any look of longing from her face, and succeeded in looking simply tired and overwhelmed. Later, as she bent over the microscope in the lab, he came in with some slides of his own. He sat on the stool beside her. When she looked up, he examined her face. 'You looked all in just now,' he said.

She shook her head. 'I'm OK,' she told him. 'I was just feeling a little—discouraged. Things just seem to get worse all the time. This woman's got a pneumococcal pneumonia now.'

She sighed, and stood up, and in a moment Richard had done the same. Wordlessly he put his arms around her and held her to him so that she could feel the warmth and the hardness of his body and his heart beating in his chest.

She couldn't stop herself—she let herself melt against him and closed her eyes. The arms around her were like the walls of a sanctuary, shutting out fear and fatigue. She wanted to stay there forever, and let all the patients die.

She sighed again. They mustn't die. And she must get back to them. He let her go, and she smiled at him, grateful for the kindness that had prompted his embrace, grateful that he had known what she needed. He smiled back, the smile she remembered from the Nuba Mountains, one that reached his clear grey eyes and lit them.

Gena returned to her patients. Thank God I'm not here alone, she thought. It occurred to her for the first time that one of them could get sick, and in the same instant she realised why it had come to her mind. Surely Richard's heart had been beating very fast when she laid her head against his chest? A moment of blind panic seized her. If he were to come down with it, she would never cope on her own. It would be chaos. She took a deep breath and remembered what her father had taught her.

'There'll be times,' he used to say, 'when you will have to tell yourself you can only do what you can.' It calmed her a little. But the fear remained in diluted form, and made her realise how much she depended on this man whom she didn't know whether to love or hate.

The following day was to be the worst. In years to come it was to retain its place as the most chaotic of Gena's career. For a start it began after a night of no sleep at all. And at six o'clock that evening, after a day in which only the most urgent tasks could be done and more were always waiting, she realised that she hadn't sat down in twenty-four hours.

Matron Potts had come to find her and tell her that a hot meal was waiting in Richard's office. She had found him there as well, already gulping it gratefully down, and she sank into a chair and wordlessly did likewise.

Sitting down was wonderful. She leant her spine

against the chair and enjoyed the luxury of it, and at the same time knew the blessed relief of kicking off her shoes. She was in the clothes she had worn yesterday, the ones she had worn to Udari her first day. The white skirt, though it fitted just as well, was spotted with blood and streaked with dirt now. A button had come off the shirt in a strategic place, and her hair was everywhere. But she didn't care. She stretched out further in the chair and swung her legs on to its neighbour, sighing with pleasure. She looked critically at her shapely brown legs.

'I'm sure to be getting varicose veins,' she said.

Richard laughed, but it sounded strained.

She looked over at him. He was pale with dark shadows under his eyes and a strange sort of look. The fear gripped Gena again that he might get sick. 'Do you feel all right?' she asked.

He raised an eyebrow quizzically. 'Do I look that bad?' he asked, and she was reassured when he smiled and his face relaxed.

She grinned. 'Do you want the truth, or a polite social lie?'

He laughed again, and it sounded normal this time. 'I think, in the interests of morale, I'd better have the lie,' he told her.

The rest of the evening was for Gena a sort of waking dream. Mechanically, she kept on with her tasks, but she felt disembodied and strangely weightless. Several times when she stood up she seemed to lose balance and the ward span round her.

'Are you all right, Gena?' Heather asked her.

'I think I'm all right,' she replied. 'But I couldn't swear to it. I don't think I could swear to anything right now. I've counted this kid's respirations three times now, and I keep losing count every time.'

'I know—I'm doing the same with the pulses. I get to sixteen and then I think, Hell, I haven't bathed this kid since yesterday, and then I'm lost.'

Gena sighed. 'It's got to stop soon. We can't go on working like this. Maybe Richard can, but I can't.'

Heather nodded. 'Yes, he's magnificent, isn't he?' she said quietly.

Something in the way she said it struck Gena. There was some undercurrent, some special significance. A proprietorial tone? Gena tried to follow the line of thought, but found she couldn't. Her brain wouldn't function.

Matron Potts came to join them. 'It must be time for you to get some sleep, Gena. We've all had some through the day, in shifts. You've had none.' Clearly she wasn't about to let one of her doctors drop in her tracks.

'I will very soon, Matron,' said Gena. 'Right after I've remembered how to count to thirty. I used to be able to do it.'

Matron gave a chuckle, but her face was concerned. The girl was about ten times tougher than she looked, but there was a limit to anyone's strength. Matron stifled a sigh. Even her own, perhaps.

But Gena battled on. There were so many tasks

she wanted to finish. There was a whole list of patients she needed to get blood and sputum samples from, to send to Khartoum in the morning. And there were some drugs to be ordered.

When Gena found herself checking and rechecking drug dosages, however, and still feeling uncertain she had got them right, she realised she would have to sleep soon.

At eleven, Richard had evidently come to the same conclusion. He came to find her. 'Things are as quiet as they'll be tonight,' he said. 'I propose we get a few hours' sleep.'

She was too tired to do anything but nod her agreement, and she let him put a hand on her arm and lead her back towards the residence.

When the nurse awoke her at four o'clock, she couldn't remember having taken her clothes off or lain on the bed. For a moment she couldn't comprehend where she was, or what this native girl should be doing waking her. But it soon came back, and she forced herself to listen to what the nurse was telling her.

There was a child who was having a convulsion. She had been fitting now for ten minutes and she was going blue. Dr Gena must come quickly.

Status epilepticus came to the surface of Gena's brain. She would need a drip if she didn't have one, and some drugs to control it. Painfully she dragged herself out of bed. She pulled her jeans on, but went in the singlet top that served as a nightie.

The little girl was flushed and hot. She continued

to fit, her eyes rolled up, her thin little limbs quaking, her breath coming in hoarse gasps.

Automatically Gena asked for oxygen and for the drug which would stop the fitting. She squirted it into the drip already in place. In minutes the child lay still, breathing shallowly and slowly now on the oxygen mask.

Gena forced her eyes to focus on the child's notes: 'Influenza, severe dehydration, chest clear. Rehydrating well with the intravenous fluids, but temperature still very high.' She listened to her chest. She had no signs of pneumonia. She looked at her tongue. It was moist. She bent the little girl's head forward, and despite the large dose of relaxant she had had, it felt stiff.

Meningitis, thought Gena. Could it follow influenza? She thought it could. But they hadn't seen any others. And if it was meningitis, was it a direct result of the virus, or a bacterial one? She knew she should know about this, but she couldn't seem to remember whether meningitis was a complication of this sort of influenza or not. Perhaps it wasn't meningitis. Perhaps it was only a febrile convulsion after all. Gena tried to steady her brain and think it through, but it seemed impossible. She couldn't think what to do. She would have to wake Richard.

The residence was deathly still, but the first light of dawn was creeping through the open window into Richard's room. He lay flung out on the bed, his shirt off and his boots, but otherwise still in his clothes.

She watched him for a moment, arrested by the sight of his sleeping face, the dark hair curling on his forehead, and the beauty of him as he lay bare, his chest rising and falling slowly. She didn't want to wake him; he had had so little sleep. The nurses had already woken him once. They'd decided to wake the doctors in turn if they needed them. He would think her an ignorant fool. He had every right to be angry.

Gena hesitated, then thought of the little girl. She didn't know what to do. She needed him.

She went to his side and bent over him, putting her hand on his shoulder. She found herself shivering a little. There was still a chill in the air, and she had very little on, just this thin singlet and nothing under it. His shoulder felt warm under her cold hand. She shook him gently and called his name.

He opened his eyes and, like her, seemed blank for a moment, then appeared to focus on her. He swept his eyes over her slowly, as though trying to place her, Gena thought.

'It's me—Gena,' she said stupidly.

His face relaxed into a smile. 'I rather thought it was,' he said, and his voice sounded hoarse from sleep.

'I'm so sorry to wake you, Richard. I just didn't know what to do, and I think it's serious.'

He continued to look at her, with a curious expression, Gena thought. Was he angry?

'I know I should know this, but I don't.' Her voice sounded small and forlorn in her ears.

It must have sounded the same to him, she thought, for all at once he had reached out and drawn her down against him, sliding his arms around behind her. She could feel the warmth of his skin through her singlet, and her cheek rested against the smoothness of his shoulder. The subtle masculine scent of him came to her, and his voice was deep and gentle in her ear, and still thick with sleep.

'That's what I'm here for,' he said. 'Did you think I'd be angry?'

Gena was wholly unprepared for the emotions that swept over her like an engulfing wave. There was a sensation of flooding warmth which somehow made it difficult to breathe and a feeling that she was melting, melting into him, becoming a part of his fragrant body forever, and she felt her heart thudding as though it would like to escape. And she knew in that instant that her heart would never escape. Whatever happened in her life from now, she loved Richard Maddison as she had never loved before, and she always would.

But she also knew that her heart was hammering, and that she had to get away. She drew back, sitting up, and he let her go.

'I'll be with you in a moment,' he said, and Gena fled from the room.

CHAPTER TEN

WHEN the epidemic was all over the town of Udari mourned its dead. A ceremony was held outside the town, and the hospital staff were invited. Here the people of Udari expressed their gratitude for what the doctors and nurses had done.

'You deserve that praise, Gena,' said Richard, as they walked back later along the dusty road.

Gena knew she had surprised him with her stamina. Today especially, dressed for the ceremony in a dress that emphasised her shapeliness, and with the golden hair waving around her face, she looked too slight and elegant to have accomplished what she had. But they all knew now exactly what steel lay within her.

She reflected that the episode of the wrong drug dose seemed now to have happened a century ago, or perhaps to some other girl. During the epidemic she had no longer had time to think about it, and now, with all those new experiences crowded into those frightful weeks, it was as though it lay covered up in their minds.

Perhaps she had atoned in Richard's eyes. For he seemed to have forgotten about it entirely. The demonstrative kindness he had shown during the height of the influenza had continued as they mopped up afterwards and worked to regain order in their little world.

It was for Gena at once a pleasure and a source of pain. It was a pleasure to feel that he liked her. It was painful to be wishing it was something more.

After the night which had brought the realisation to her brain of what her heart already knew, she had been grateful in one way for the pace of work in the hospital. It stopped her thinking about Richard. When work slowed, however, she was free to feel the full force of it.

Gazing out over the flat plain to the Nuba Mountains, at the quiet end of the veranda where the others didn't go, Gena let her mind wander over it. Dislike had turned to liking in those hills, but when had it turned to love? Was there a moment, a space of time when he had become so dear to her? She had flashes of him, like snapshots from an album. Richard leaning over a sick child, his face tender. Richard with an expression of irony and fun, having made a dry joke. Richard with his shirt off, digging sand in the sun, seeming inexhaustible. Richard thoughtful. Richard sad. And the sweetest of all, Richard sensing her tiredness and anxiety, and offering her his comforting arms.

Perhaps love was like a jigsaw. The pieces were all there from the beginning, and gradually they were put together till the last one fitted into place and the picture was revealed.

And how she loved him now. Had she ever loved

Peter? Not like this. Not with this aching longing,
this tender joy, this flooding emotion that left her
breathless and weak. Gena leaned her head back in
the chair and closed her eyes for a moment. The
hills were dark now, the sun hiding behind them.
The air was still and sultry, the song of crickets
floating up to her. It was such a difficult emotion to
hide. Gena had always been an open person. From
childhood affectionate, she was quick to show
warmth and friendship. It was foreign to her to feel
something like this and to stuff it down and hide it
away.

But hide it she must. For there was no likelihood
of Richard's returning her feelings, she thought. For
a start, she was so much younger than he, and more
than once he had laughed at her childlike naïveté.
And even if he could find that appealing or something, thought Gena wistfully, those blood tubes
and, even more, that drug order would always stand
between them. It was not to be expected that
someone like him would care for someone capable
of telling cowardly lies, even if he had forgiven her
enough to be friendly. That was, after all, what he
believed of her.

Gena knew that she herself could never love
anyone who did that sort of thing. Maybe if those
things hadn't happened, she thought wistfully, and
maybe if I were just a little bit more sophisticated. . . But it wasn't so. They had happened, and
she was just a simple young Australian girl from a
country town.

The days that followed were difficult for Gena. Things were a little better when Angus and Jonathan returned from the west. Of course, there was Jonathan to hide it from as well then, and he was the most acute of them all where Gena was concerned. But this disadvantage was far outweighed by the advantage of having him there to distract her and absorb her attention. Had she been totally honest with herself, she would also have been forced to admit that he provided a handy means of throwing any who suspected how her feelings really lay well and truly off the scent.

They became, therefore, constant companions, and Gudwe at least was pleased to see his plans being forwarded.

Still, in guarding herself against showing her feelings to the embarrassment of all concerned, Gena was a little quieter than usual. There were varying opinions among the others as to the cause of this.

'Pretty nasty experience for a young woman, that epidemic,' said Angus. 'So many people dying in front of you.'

'Probably just worn out,' said Jonathan. 'She's been worked into the ground.'

Richard had another idea. 'Perhaps she's had enough of life out here. After all, it's not what a— an attractive young woman would choose to do for a lifetime. It's inevitable that she'll want to go back to her own people and life. She's surprised me in maintaining her enthusiasm for it as long as she has.'

Matron Potts, sitting back in her chair in the shadows, smiled to herself, but didn't give an opinion.

'Want to come to Khartoum with me in the plane?' Richard asked Gena in the morning. 'I'm taking that woman with the heart trouble, but there'll be time to see the sights.'

Gena hesitated a moment. Her heart cried out 'Oh, yes!' To spend a day in his company, exploring the city of Khartoum—what an unexpected pleasure! But her head must rule her. She must stay in control of her feelings, and not let him guess. The more time she spent with him, and especially time alone, the more opportunity there would be for her feelings to grow and deepen, and the greater the chance too that she would give herself away.

Richard could not have missed her hesitation. And he looked at her for a moment, then turned away. 'I would send Jonathan if I could, and let you go with him. I'm afraid it's not possible. I have business there.'

Gena's heart lurched, and she felt herself redden. Did he suspect already, then? Did he too feel that she oughtn't spend too much time in his company?

'I think it would do you good,' he said, and waited for her answer.

She struggled to be casual. He had only offered her a day's sightseeing in Khartoum. She mustn't behave as though it meant any more to her than that. If he suspected that his young assistant was overly fond of him, and about to become a problem, she must convince him that he was wrong. She could handle it.

'That would be nice,' she said lightly. 'I've wanted to see Khartoum. Jonathan's told me what an intriguing place it is.'

Richard grunted assent, and seemed satisfied.

The following morning, in honour of the occasion, she abandoned her khaki drill shorts and wore a dress that elicited tribute from Jonathan and Angus.

'Oh, do be gentlemen!' she said, laughing at them.

'My dear girl, hardly gentlemanly to ignore such a vision of loveliness,' said Angus.

'Oh, rot!' said Gena.

'No, you look lovely, Gena,' said Heather, and Gena turned to smile at her gratefully. The girl smiled back, but her face was strained. The epidemic has taken its toll of us all, Gena thought.

Richard flicked his eyes over her too, but silently, when she joined him for the ride to the airstrip, and Gena suddenly felt unsure of herself. Maybe she shouldn't have worn the dress, or perhaps she should have worn one that showed less of her legs.

Richard, she was uneasily aware, looked wonderful. He too had abandoned his workaday khaki, and was tall and suntanned in cool light linen. He tossed his jacket on to the seat in front in the aircraft and eased himself into the place next to Gena.

'These aircraft are abominable for anyone over five feet ten,' he remarked.

She only smiled, already feeling misgivings about this trip. Just to have him sitting next to her in the confines of the aircraft, with his arm touching her shoulder, and his good-looking face not far from hers, was enough to elevate her pulse-rate. She had better look out of the window.

Richard himself was occupied to some extent with his patient during the flight. The seats on the other side of the aircraft had been removed to make a space for the stretcher, and an African woman lay there, her eyes wide with apprehension. She had seen an aeroplane before, as a glittering, droning spot overhead in the hard blue sky, but never had she been in one.

Richard spoke to her comfortingly, explaining what was happening. She smiled weakly up at him, keeping her eyes on him as he settled back in his seat for take-off as though his face held the magic that would ensure their safety. And when finally they touched down again, and were driven in the ambulance to the hospital, she was distressed to be left by him.

Khartoum, Gena decided, was like a teeming anthill. Even in the worst of the midday heat, the streets and bazaars were thronged with people. They surged along wide boulevards and streamed down narrow alleys. They gathered around the market stalls and squatted in groups on the roadsides, begging. The dust, the filth, the colour, the noise, the movement combined for Gena in a kaleidoscopic pattern which fascinated and which she didn't want to leave.

'There's a place over here where we can get a cool drink,' Richard told her, obviously less enthusiastic than she, having seen it all before.

Gena allowed him to take her arm and steer her through the crowd to a dim hostelry with a tiled courtyard away from the noise. They sat in the shade there, Richard with a sigh of relief.

Gena sat with her head on her hands and her elbows on the table, and thought of what she had seen. 'Imagine having the sheer energy to keep afloat on that thronging tide of humanity,' she murmured, half to herself. 'I think I'd just sink and be trampled on.' She looked up and saw Richard watching her with a smile. 'Do you know what I mean?' she asked him.

'Exactly,' he said. 'But I'm not sure you would sink, Gena. You have the same exuberant life in you that keeps these people going.'

They sat in the shade of the baobab tree and sipped their drinks in a kind of companionable languor. Gena could not prevent herself from studying him. She did so covertly, and tried to imagine that she had never met him and was seeing him here for the first time. What would she have thought of him? She would notice him, that was for sure. He leaned back in his chair with an air of repose, his long powerful legs stretched out before him, one muscular brown arm, shirtsleeves rolled up, resting on the table-top. His face was strong and brown and intelligent, and the sight of it brought again those feelings unbidden to Gena that left her feeling dizzy and breathless. But, most of the visitors to the place being male, it was perhaps not surprising that they didn't spend as much time in regarding Richard as they did in staring at the lovely girl at his side whose hair framed an angel's face in golden waves.

In the afternoon, as the day grew cooler and the shadows lengthened, Richard bought Gena a woven scarf to wear on her head and they visited a magnificent mosque with golden sculptures and mosaics a hundred years old. They climbed to the top and looked out over Khartoum at its minarets and domes, and felt far away from the squalor of the bazaar. At dusk the prayer calls began, and echoed through the quietening city. Gena and Richard sat on a seat in the garden of a temple and listened to them in the gathering dusk.

'I'm glad I didn't miss this,' she said.

'Mm.' His voice was quiet. 'You look a little more relaxed than you did.'

'It's seeing life in perspective. We can get so preoccupied with our own concerns, and pine for things we can't have. And then you see these people surviving on so little, but somehow joyful still.'

'Their faith helps them,' he said, and Gena nodded. It was true—they bent to the will of Allah. 'Do you want to stay tonight?' he asked suddenly.

She felt her heart quicken at the prospect, and before any sensible consideration could take place in her mind, had cried, 'Oh, yes!'

He laughed at her enthusiasm, and she blushed a little. 'Very well,' he said. 'We'll radio them from the hospital.'

A dozen taxi-drivers fought for their custom in the square, and the winner beamed as he helped them into the ancient battered car. He drove as though confident that Allah was watching over him, turning round to talk to them as he sped through the streets, and only occasionally bestowing his gaze on the road ahead.

'Do you have many accidents?' Gena asked conversationally.

'Oh, yes, miss,' he replied. 'Many, many accidents.'

She met Richard's eyes in the back and convulsed in silent laughter.

At the hospital, he insisted on waiting to take them back, though Richard wanted to pay a visit to the Udari woman to see that she had settled in. It was no trouble to wait, he assured them.

'Oh, God!' groaned Gena, when they were out of earshot. 'Do they kill many passengers?'

'Hardly any,' replied Richard gravely, his eyes twinkling.

The hospital gave them rooms to stay in, though Gena would secretly have liked to stay in a Khartoum hotel and brave the bed-bugs.

They ate at one, anyway. It was an establishment of fading opulence, with a battalion of brightly dressed Arab waiters, but very few guests. Richard and Gena dined in solitary state on a terrace over-looking the lights of the city and drinking in the heady scent of a nearby frangipani tree.

'This is lovely,' sighed Gena as she picked up the liqueur the waiter had left her.

'Mmm,' murmured Richard. 'In all the years I've spent out here, I've never done this myself.'

'Why not?' she asked.

He seemed to consider awhile. 'I don't suppose there's been anyone to do it with,' he said.

Gena wondered for the first time what a man so—well, masculine—did out here alone. Was he lonely? Did he miss women? Was there, from time to time, someone at the hospital? She wanted to ask. Had he ever been in love?

Schooling her voice to be casual, she asked him, 'You've never been married, Richard?'

He shook his head. 'I—considered it, at one stage. But it wouldn't have suited her here.'

His work came first, then. It was as she had thought.

He looked at Gena. 'What about you, Gena? Is there someone waiting for you?'

She shook her head. 'There was someone who refused to wait. But I've since realised that it was a very good thing.'

He sat back in his chair seeming to examine her face, and Gena felt the now familiar tightness in her chest. 'I see,' he said at last.

Gena hoped that he didn't. She didn't want him

to know that she had only learned what love was really about through loving him.

'You won't be alone for long, though,' he said.

She wanted to tell him not to be so sure. For how could she ever find a man to measure up to him? It was going to take a lot of doing. Perhaps she would never find one to love like this, and who also loved her.

Her face was sad for a moment. 'I don't want to be alone forever.' It was a non-committal reply.

'No.' He smiled. 'That would be a waste.'

It was a compliment, and Gena smiled in acknowledgement.

'You need someone strong, though,' he continued. 'Someone as strong as you, or stronger. Otherwise you'd find him leaning on you, and you won't respect that.'

Gena looked at him. What was he trying to tell her?

'You—you're fond of Jonathan,' he said tentatively.

Her eyes widened. Had she fooled everyone as well as that? 'Yes, I am fond of him,' she said, keeping her voice neutral. 'He's a nice boy.'

'No more?' asked Richard, his voice low.

She *had* fooled them as well as that. He was as far from guessing her secret as he could possibly be. It was safe to tell the truth.

'No more,' she said, smiling. 'He's like a brother.'

Richard's reaction was strange, she thought. He sat completely still. He was silent. Only his eyes responded to what she had said, the expression in them changing to something that she could not interpret.

He took a mouthful of his drink, at length, but still sat silently, appearing lost in thought.

'Those flowers smell so wonderful,' Gena said to change the subject, but Richard didn't respond to the conversational opening.

'What do you want to do in medicine?' he asked abruptly. 'A general practice? A specialty?'

She frowned as she looked out over the city, thinking. 'I—I don't know,' she said. 'Somehow, at the moment, I can't seem to imagine myself anywhere but here, in the Sudan.'

'It's a hard life here,' he said. 'You must be getting tired of it by now.'

She widened her eyes in surprise. 'No!' she cried. 'I'm not tired of it at all. I love it here. It matters.' She frowned in concentration. 'I could go back to Australia and become one more GP in one more suburban surgery. But it wouldn't matter whether I was there or not. It's the same with a specialty. One more specialist for people to choose from in a rich, well-fed society that has boundless choices already.'

He looked at her with an arrested expression. 'You're not thinking of staying here?' he asked.

She returned his gaze steadily. 'Why not?' she asked.

'The heat, the dust, the loneliness, the fatigue. . . I should think you would know by now.'

She laughed. 'Yes, I know.' And she reflected that

she did know, now. Until she had said it she hadn't realised herself that she was considering staying in the Sudan. But the more she thought about it the more right it seemed, even if she had to work in a different part of it from Richard. That would probably be better for her, she reflected. And now his expression was as unreadable as ever. Did he think her a romantic fool, who would get over the idea? Did he welcome it? Did he still consider her unsuitable?

They lingered together over their coffee and liqueurs, not speaking now, but lost in their own thoughts. Only Richard a couple of times looked as though he might speak, but appeared to change his mind on seeing the pondering face of the girl.

An amount of good-natured ribbing had to be endured on the return of the travellers to Udari.

'Never thought we'd see you again, did we, Jonathan? Thought you'd eloped.'

'Yes, and I was very disappointed in you, Gena. I'd thought you had better taste.' Jonathan gave Richard a cheeky grin.

Even Matron joined in the fun, and only Pauline and Heather forbore to comment. Heather looked more tired than when Gena had gone away, and she suddenly felt that Heather would have benefited more from the trip than she herself. It made her feel guilty.

'Well, come on,' said Jonathan. 'What did you do

there, while we were stuck out here doing all the work?'

'Oh, poor lad,' murmured Richard, and Jonathan grinned again.

'We strolled in the bazaar, and Richard bought me a scarf, and we went to a mosque and sat in a garden, and then we had a sumptuous dinner on a moonlit terrace,' said Gena. 'Oh, and we took the woman to the hospital,' she added as a guilty afterthought.

'I'm surprised you remembered to do that,' said Jonathan, and Gena laughed.

'Just what you needed, my dear,' said Angus. 'You were looking a little tired, but now you look radiant.'

It was true. And she felt wonderful. But she refused to examine too closely the reason. Perhaps she unconsciously feared that it had too much to do with the way that Richard had silently taken her arm after dinner for the walk back to the square, and the way he had steadied her with his hand as they were thrown about in the taxi. To hope too much, Gena knew, could be very dangerous.

Gudwe brought them cool drinks on a tray, and she swung round to take one. As she did so she caught sight of Pauline. The girl was standing to one side of her. She was motionless, with her eyes fixed on Gena. They were burning, Gena thought.

It startled her. She stared back at Pauline for a moment, the wide blue eyes meeting the glittering black ones. Then Pauline turned silently and went inside.

While the others were discussing the mosques of Khartoum, Gena was sipping her lemonade and wondering whether it was the ice-cold drink or Pauline which made her feel like shivering.

CHAPTER ELEVEN

THE next few days were among the happiest that Gena could remember. For a wild hope was growing within her, nourished by every smile and friendly word that Richard gave her as they saw patients in the clinic and did their rounds in the hospital. She didn't quite know why she had begun to hope that Richard might care for her. She knew when it had started. That was in Khartoum.

Perhaps it had been only the seductive scent of the frangipani and the stars. Perhaps she was mad. But it had seemed to her as he took her arm and walked with her after dinner in the moonlight that there was a different quality in his touch and a new, more caressing tone to his voice. Such a hope, once sprung up, was difficult to choke off even with large self-servings of common sense, Gena found. She told herself to be careful, but her heart ignored her.

And then all at once it happened. They were in the clinic, putting away the patients' files after the morning's work. She filed the last cards and pushed the drawer shut, then turned to find him standing there close to her. Her heart thudded. Richard reached out for her and slowly pulled her to him. He folded his arms around her as he had done before, but this time it was no fatherly hug he was giving her. He pressed her body tightly against his and brought his lips down on hers in a kiss that seemed to fill Gena with liquid fire. Her heart pounded; it was hard to breathe, but she didn't care. He moved his lips on hers and she felt a weakness flood her. His hard body was against her, and his lips continued to move on her mouth; and she answered him with every part of her.

Finally he freed her lips, but kept his arms around her, looking down at her face, his breathing ragged.

'Oh, Richard!' she cried hoarsely. She was trembling.

A door slamming nearby made her jump, and Richard let her go. It was just as well. A nurse burst into the clinic.

'Oh, Dr Maddison,' she exclaimed. 'Can you come? A man has cut his fingers off!'

Quickly he nodded and turned for a moment to Gena. 'I'll see you later,' he said softly.

When he was gone, Gena sat on the edge of the desk and took several deep breaths. When her brain began to function once more, there was only one thought there. Let it mean that he loves me. Oh, please! Let it mean that he loves me. She washed her face in the clinic sink and looked at herself in the mirror above it. Her face was still flushed. She thought it looked quite pretty. Oh, don't let it just be that, she silently prayed. A man alone in the desert. A passably pretty girl. A physical attraction.

She loved him so desperately—and now she had

told him so. Her lips and her body, her complete surrender must have told him so.

She straightened her skirt to walk back to the residence and to wait for the answer. The residence was empty, to Gena's relief, and she remembered the others had gone into town. She had a shower and washed her hair and changed her clothes, as much to pass the time as anything. She wondered if she should have a nap, but thought that she'd never be able to sleep, so she sat on the end of the bed instead and dried her hair in the sunlight that streamed through the window.

The sound of Richard's unmistakable tread in the sitting-room made her drop her brush. Her heart pounded once more, and she got up slowly, smoothing her skirt. As she did, her eyes caught something on the bed.

She leant to have a closer look. What was that? It was a brown thing, like a leaf, beneath the mosquito net, half covered by the sheet.

She pulled back the sheet to see and before she could stop herself let out a scream, a long loud scream of pure instinctive horror, as she realised what it was.

It was a scorpion.

The door burst open as she stood there. 'What is it?' cried Richard.

And she pointed, her face pale. He looked where she was pointing and became completely still. The deadly scorpion crawled along the sheet. It was well and truly alive.

'You didn't touch it?' Richard's voice sounded breathless.

'No,' Gena's was hoarse. 'I was sitting on the end of the bed and I saw something. I got up to look.'

He let his breath out. 'All right,' he said. 'Go and sit in the sitting-room. I'll get rid of it.'

'Richard, don't. . .'

'Get bitten?' he said. 'Hardly.'

Gena had largely composed herself when Angus and Jonathan arrived back from town a few minutes later.

'Hello, there,' said Jonathan. 'Had a nice day?'

'Apart from scorpions in my bed, lovely,' she said calmly.

The two men stared at her.

'Well, OK, I'm exaggerating,' she confessed. 'There was only one.'

Angus looked at Jonathan and then at Richard as he came back inside.

'What did you do with it?' asked Gena.

'Not something the conservationists would approve of,' he replied.

'Wait a minute!' cried Angus. 'Is this—was there really a scorpion in the house?'

Richard nodded grimly.

'Bless me!' Angus ejaculated. 'Never known that to happen here.'

'No,' said Richard. 'Very bad luck.' His words seemed somehow pointed.

'If mosquito netting won't keep them out,' said Gena, 'what will?'

'You don't mean to say it was really in your bed?' demanded Jonathan.

'I do mean to say so,' said Gena with emphasis. 'And I take exception to it.'

'But——' Angus began, but went no further as Richard gave a just perceptible shake of his head. The two men stood looking at one another, the younger one grim, and something very like fear dawning in the eyes of the elder.

A few minutes later they had walked outside. Richard spoke first, in a quiet voice.

'Have you ever known a scorpion to crawl into somebody's bed?'

'No,' said Angus. 'Never.'

'Or anyway, under a mosquito net?'

'It's impossible,' said Angus. 'They can't even get into the house here.'

'That's what I thought.' They looked at one another for a moment, unwilling to accept the logical conclusion.

'It only leaves one thought,' said Angus slowly.

'Exactly.' Richard's voice was grim. 'Who put it there? And why?'

Angus shook his head. 'I can't believe it.'

'I don't want to believe it,' said Richard. 'But I can't think of any other explanation.'

'Why would anyone want to do that to Gena?' cried Angus. 'Of all people. . .' His voice trailed away.

'It rather reminds one of something else, doesn't it?' asked Richard.

'What's that?'

'You will remember that mistake Gena made with the drug dose,' Richard said deliberately. 'She was certain she'd written twenty milligrams. I couldn't accept that—because the only other explanation was that someone else had altered it. And then, as now, I couldn't think of anyone who would do that, or why they should do it.' Angus stared at him. 'I escaped from that dilemma by blaming Gena.' He paused. 'Perhaps I was wrong.'

'It's fantastic to think that someone would alter a drug order to produce a fatal overdose,' said Angus slowly. 'But it's just as fantastic to think that someone has played such an irresponsible joke on Gena. I see what you mean.'

'I'm not even certain whether I see it as you do. An irresponsible joke? Something to scare her, you think? But there's no one around here who isn't perfectly aware that a good bite from a scorpion would kill Gena.'

Angus's face was filled with horror. 'Good God, Richard! Are you really saying it was meant to kill her?'

'If she'd lain on the bed for a rest, it would have! Suppose,' Richard continued, 'suppose that Gena *was* right about the pethidine? Go back further, and suppose she was right about those damn blood tubes?' Angus gave an exclamation, as he remembered. 'Then someone has made three attempts to hurt her. The first one was designed to get her into trouble. The second was to implicate her in the death of a child. The third. . .' He didn't need to finish.

'My God, Richard,' Angus groaned. 'I believe you're right. I never could imagine Gena making that mistake—she just doesn't do things like that.'

'No,' said Richard softly. 'I think you're right. And I think I was very wrong. I wish to God I'd listened to her.'

'What are we going to do? Who have we got here that crazy? And why Gena? Everyone here loves her!' Angus exclaimed. 'She's a grand girl!'

Richard smiled wryly at his friend. 'Someone either doesn't think so, or doesn't care about that. Someone doesn't want her here.'

'I can't think of anyone!' Angus declared. 'Can you?'

But Richard didn't answer. He was frowning while he stared into space. He appeared to be thinking very hard.

'One thing's certain,' he said at last. 'I'm not waiting for the fourth attempt to get rid of her.'

Angus could only agree.

'And I'm going to get to the bottom of it, whatever I do.'

And at last, just as the sunset was fading into night, Richard joined Gena where she sat alone at the far end of the veranda. He sat in the old wicker chair beside her, and was silent for a long while, and Gena sat silently too, her heart engaged in a rapid rhythm of anticipation.

When finally he spoke, she was totally unprepared for his words.

'Gena, you're going to have to leave here, as soon as arrangements can be made.'

She jerked round to look at him. 'Leave here?' she echoed in astonishment.

In the gathering darkness, he nodded. 'That scorpion was no accident. They can't get into this house. They don't crawl under secured mosquito netting to get into people's beds.' He turned his face towards her. 'Do you see what I'm saying? It was put there.'

Despite the warmth of the night, she shivered. 'I wondered,' she said simply.

'So you see, someone is trying to hurt you. And I think they've tried before.' He paused a moment. 'I'm sorry I doubted you, Gena.'

She knew what he meant. 'But I don't see why I should leave here,' she said. 'Just because someone tries to scare me.'

'No, Gena, it was more serious than that. If you'd got into that bed and been bitten, it would have killed you. Your small body would never withstand a good bite from one.'

'I almost did,' she replied. 'I almost lay down for a sleep. But I would have seen it, I'm sure.'

'You must leave,' he repeated. 'There's a place in the hospital at Khartoum. . .'

Gena thought. Someone was certainly trying to frighten her, just as they tried before to make trouble for her. And she thought she knew who it was. It was someone with a crazy devotion to

Richard. Someone who had tried to destroy the friendship between Gena and Richard on two occasions, and who, having failed, had resorted to more desperate measures.

One face swam before Gena's eyes, the dark eyes blazing. It had to be Pauline.

Pauline loved Richard—Gena was sure of it. Pauline had access to the patients' charts and could have changed that drug dose. Pauline was the one who had 'found' the child and given the alarm. She had not meant to kill the child, but she was prepared to run a considerable risk.

And she had not meant to kill Gena, Gena felt certain. It was only meant to frighten her. Pauline was a strange woman, with a deep attachment to Richard, and she saw Gena, rightly or wrongly, as someone who had got too close to him. No doubt she wanted her to leave, and thought that the scorpion might do it.

But try as she might, for all Pauline's peculiar quality, Gena could not cast her in the role of cold-blooded killer. She was just crazy enough to take risks, that was all. Gena would have it out with the girl. One way or another, they would resolve it. And Pauline wouldn't dare try anything else once Gena had confronted her.

'Can you think of anyone who would do this?' Richard was asking.

Gena was silent a moment. There was no need to confide in Richard. She was confident she could

handle Pauline herself, and put a stop to this dangerous nonsense for good.

'No,' she said firmly.

'No one whom you've inadvertently offended?
Who has shown they dislike you, or resent you?'

'No one at all,' she repeated.

He sighed.

'I won't leave, though, Richard. I won't let—this
person—drive me away.'

But Richard's voice came to her, and it was
implacable. 'Gena, I'm going to insist.'

She felt her throat tighten. He sounded as though
he meant it. He really wanted her to leave. Even if
he was concerned for her safety, how could he, after
today? She turned to him and said softly, 'What
about—earlier today?'

He was silent a moment, and then his words
stunned her. 'Perhaps that's another reason.'

Gena felt it like a blow. She kept her voice even
through effort. 'What do you mean?' she said.

He was staring straight ahead. 'It should never
have happened,' he said. 'I was weak. You're very
attractive.'

The blood rushed to Gena's face and flamed there.
She felt a terrible anguish envelop her. He didn't
love her. She didn't speak; she couldn't have trusted
her voice. If she had opened her mouth she would
have sobbed. It hadn't been love that had motivated
him at all. And he knew now that she loved him.
She had told him so, as clearly as words, in that kiss.

He didn't want the complication. He didn't want

her love. He wanted her to go away. It hurt her with a physical pain.

Gradually as she fought for control and clarity of mind she gained it. She drew her dignity around her. Very well: she loved him and he didn't love her. Did he think she was going to fall about sobbing and creep away in the morning, forgetting her responsibilities like a hurt child? Did he think she was going to importune him and make his life a misery? Did he think she lacked the character to take the blow, swallow her disappointment and go on in a civilised and adult manner?

Well, she would show him something! She would feel the real pain of this later, when she was alone. But she wasn't so weak or lacking in pride that she would let that stop her from doing the job she had chosen right up to the end of her contract.

She took a deep breath and schooled her voice to calmness. 'Then we shall have to be stronger. Or I'll be strong enough for both of us.'

The look he gave her might have been admiration. Whatever it was, it was twisting the knife in her to meet those grey eyes. She had to look away, or let him see how much it hurt, and she was not going to do that. She was going to make it clear that he need have no fears that she would make life difficult for him.

'We'll put it behind us,' she went on. 'I don't see that it need affect our professional relationship.'

He was silent a moment, and, had Gena dared to look, she might have seen an extraordinary mix of emotions in his face. But at length he spoke with decision. 'I'm afraid I don't see things as you do. I've made up my mind, Gena. I'm not prepared to take the risk of having you remain here.'

A sudden anger rose in her. What was he talking about? The risk to her, from her unidentified enemy? Or the risk to him, from her? Was she not showing him that she could behave like an adult?

'The risk is mine!' she flared. 'And I'm not running away from my job!'

An answering anger began to show in him. 'You're being remarkably foolish. Your safety has been threatened—you don't know by whom. You don't know what will happen next. I'm not about to sit by and——'

'I'm not going,' she answered flatly.

She felt his temper flare. 'Then I'm ordering you to!' he blazed. 'I'm terminating your employment.'

Gena's eyes flashed. 'You have no such right!' she flung. 'You didn't employ me—the Board did.'

'Then the Board will sack you,' he snapped.

'On what grounds?' she demanded.

He leant forward and gripped her arm savagely. 'On any grounds I like,' he grated. 'On the grounds that you're too stupid to know what's good for you.'

Gena flung off his arm and sprang to her feet. She was furious now. 'You've wanted to get rid of me ever since I got here!' she cried. 'You were prejudiced against me from the beginning, and you weren't even willing to give me a chance. Now you're afraid I may embarrass you. Well, don't worry, Dr Maddison, I won't languish after you. I don't even like you!' She turned on her heel and strode away.

And later, lying face down on her bed, she reflected on how strange it was that not liking a person couldn't stop you loving them.

There was only one consolation to the whole wretched business, and that was that no one had been around to hear them. It was a long time before Gena slept, and it wasn't fear of scorpions that kept her awake. She almost felt she would have welcomed one. It was the promise of happiness so cruelly withdrawn that hurt the most. She had thought that it was a loving kiss Richard had given her. She had deluded herself. It was a kiss of physical need. With a sob she thought that she could almost settle for that now if just a little caring went with it. But that ever-present critic inside her told her that was non-sense, she could never settle for that.

When she fell asleep at last she dreamed of Pauline Hickey. And, strangely, it wasn't an unpleasant dream. She was sick in a hospital bed and Pauline was looking after her, her large dark eyes watching over her. Then suddenly Pauline stood up and reached out her hand to something on the counterpane. She closed her hand around it, then held it out for Gena to see. A scorpion rested in the palm of her hand.

'I'll put it in the jar with the others,' she said kindly, 'then it can't hurt you.'

Gena awoke at the end of the dream, remembering it vividly. She had felt no fear. In fact, she had

felt that Pauline was there protecting her. It struck
Gena as strange for a moment that she didn't feel
afraid. Why did she not feel like running away, as
Richard had wanted? Pauline had actually put that
deadly thing in her bed. Why didn't she feel that she
was in any real danger from her? Did she know her
that well? Sighing, she stretched out further and fell
asleep again before any answer presented itself.

CHAPTER TWELVE

WHEN Gena awoke in the morning, her grief flooded over her anew.

She lay there miserably, feeling unequal to the day before her and wondering whether Richard would really put his threat of sacking her into action. In the clear light of day she was not so certain that he wasn't right anyway. Not because of any danger to her. Whatever happened, she had made up her mind to speak to Pauline this morning. She was sure after what she had to say that Pauline would never contemplate actions so crazy again.

But Richard wanted her to leave. He would be more comfortable if she were in Khartoum, or back in Australia. It was his hospital. Was it fair of her to want to stay? Or was that a rationalisation? Was she in fact doing what she had been determined not to do? Funking it. Running away because she hadn't the strength to face up to her disappointment and see the job through.

Maybe that wasn't so despicable, anyway. For wouldn't she feel the pain of her hopeless love every time she saw him? Could she really blame herself for wishing to escape that? Questions without answers, she thought hopelessly. She had no idea what to do.

She took as much time as she could about getting

up and dressing this morning. It was Richard's day
for the outpatients' clinic, not hers, and she was
hoping that he and Pauline would have gone off to
start it by the time she arrived at the breakfast table.
She would have to face him, she knew. But not just
yet.

Angus was alone in the dining-room when she got
there. Gena knew she couldn't eat, but she poured
herself a cup of tea and sat down to drink it. He
folded up his journal.

'Hello, my dear. Did you get any sleep after all
that unpleasantness yesterday?'

'Oh, yes,' Gena tried to say brightly, but she
couldn't manage it. He was so obviously concerned
for her, and looking at her so kindly and with such
affection across the table, that he accomplished what
cross words couldn't have done. Her self-control
crumbled. She bent her head and covered her eyes
with her hand, and sobbed.

For a moment he looked nonplussed, but in
another second he was at her side, hugging her and
murmuring inarticulate noises of sympathy and apology combined.

'Oh, Angus,' she was crying, 'he wants me to
leave!'

'I know, I know, my dear. It's safer. But it won't
be for long, you'll see. We'll find who played such a
nasty joke on you, send them packing in no time at
all. Richard's making enquiries already, and he's a
very determined chap.' This didn't seem to stop her
sobbing a bit, so he tried again. 'You see, you can

come back then. It'll be just like before, only no more unpleasantness.'

'Oh, Angus, I can't,' she cried. 'I can't come back. You don't know!' She choked on a sob for a moment, then went on, 'He doesn't want me to, Angus. He wants me to leave. I—I-like him too much, and he knows it, and he doesn't want me here because of that.'

There was silence for a moment from Angus as he took her words in, and when he spoke next, it was in a different tone, a tone which carried real grief.

'My dear girl,' he said gruffly, 'I—I'm sorry—I had no idea. I—my God! The stupid fellow!'

This surprised Gena sufficiently to stop her sobbing and make her look up. Angus was looking at her with a rueful sympathy. Perhaps there was even a little anger mirrored in his face. He spoke gently but with conviction. 'Then he's a very great fool, Gena. You're just exactly what he's always needed, and he's running away from it.' He made a noise of disgust. 'I don't understand him. Only—I suppose I've seen it before. His work has always come first. He refuses to have anything interfere with it. There was a girl before—oh, years back now. Just before he came out here. He broke it off.'

Angus sighed. 'Well, I'll be honest. In that case, he may have been right—she wasn't the sort for out here. And he would come out here. But you— you're perfect! You love it here, don't you?'

Dumbly, Gena nodded, the tears welling up again.

'He just doesn't feel—the right things,' she managed.

Angus looked at her with pain on his kindly face. 'Doesn't want to, more like, my dear. You see, I think that's the way he is. Medicine comes first. Nothing must distract him or get in the way. . .'

Gena supposed she understood. It was what she had thought at times herself.

'Perhaps. . .' He was hesitant. 'Perhaps it would be better if you did go, then,' he said at last. 'I'm so fond of you, my dear. I'd hate to see you stay here and be hurt.'

'Oh, Angus, it's running away, isn't it?' she said miserably. 'It's cowardly. I thought I could stay here and face it, but now, I don't know. . .'

'Nonsense,' he said gruffly. 'Nothing cowardly about it. A warm-hearted girl like you, Gena—too painful for you to stop here in these circumstances. You're asking too much of yourself. We'll get another doctor, though they won't be as good. You have to do what's best for you, not stay here for the sake of the job and be hurt. Would you go to Khartoum?' he asked.

She shook her head. 'No. If I leave here, I'll go home to my family.'

He nodded, understanding.

'Oh, Angus, but when I think of saying goodbye, I just can't stand it!'

He hugged her tightly while she wept.

Gena recovered enough at length for her to want him to leave her alone to think things out. He was

going to spend the morning with Jonathan at
Tempulu village just to the north. They wouldn't be
back till two or three o'clock, and Gena was glad.
The fewer people around this morning the better.
She went over to the wards and was grateful to find
that there was nothing for her to do there, so she
returned to her room to sit at the window which
gave on to the western plain, and to think.

Maybe Angus was right. Maybe it wasn't cowardly
to leave. If what he said about Richard was true,
and he knew him better than anyone, then it was the
right thing to do. For if Richard wanted medicine to
come first in his life, if he wanted no distractions,
then that was his choice. She had no right to remain
there and get in his way.

The more she thought about it, the more inescap-
able the conclusion became. She would have to leave
Udari. And the Sudan.

Dr Lamb had been right about his daughter pos-
sessing decision. Once she had made up her mind, it
was not her way to flinch from doing what was
necessary. Slowly and deliberately, Gena began to
fold the clothes that were in her drawers and pile
them on her bed. She would leave today. The
decision taken, there was no reason for delay.

She planned as she packed. The supply plane
would come at four o'clock and leave for Khartoum
at four-thirty. A truck would go from the hospital to
meet it, she would be on the truck.

Elinor Potts and Heather were in the wards, and
the other nurses; she could say goodbye to them this

morning. And Gudwe—poor old Gudwe. He would be sorry. Her face softened as she thought of looking for him to say goodbye, but she willed herself not to cry again.

Pauline and Richard would be back at lunchtime. Pauline. She must still have that chat with Pauline before she went—for Pauline's own sake.

She tried hard not to think of saying goodbye to Richard. She knew she must, but she would not think of it beforehand. She would stumble through it somehow at the time.

And Jonathan and Angus. Such good friends, they'd become. She would miss them both. There would just be time to say her goodbyes to them, perhaps to exchange addresses with Jonathan, to promise to write. . .

The tears would stay away no more, and for a while she couldn't see the bag she was packing.

Gudwe was in the kitchen. Gena parked her bag against the wall, and told him. 'I have to leave, Gudwe—today.'

'What for?' he demanded with his usual direct-ness, but didn't let her tell him. 'No, no, you safe here now. I watching you. Last night, sleep outside your door.'

'Oh, Gudwe, did you?'

'Of course,' was his reply. 'You not going. Richard finding bad person. I making magic for him.'

Gena was shaking her head. 'It's not just that, Gudwe,' she told him carefully. 'It's something else too—another reason. I have to leave, Gudwe—today.'

She saw that she had convinced him that she meant what she said. He stopped speaking, and gazed at her sorrowfully. Finally he spoke, and his voice was a whisper.

'I am not happy,' he said.

'I—I'll ask you to put my bag aboard the truck, Gudwe. I'll go in the truck to the plane this afternoon. What time does the driver go?' Silently, he held up four fingers. 'I'll say goodbye now, Gudwe. Don't—don't come to see me off at four. I can't bear goodbyes. And—you've been such a good friend to me. . .'

She left as the African pressed his hand to his eyes.

Taking leave of Heather and Matron and the rest of the nursing staff was hardly less difficult. But at least no explanations were necessary. They seemed to accept the scorpion as sufficient reason.

'I don't blame you,' said Heather. 'I'd be going too. If it'd been me, I would have left last night. You were brave sleeping in your bed, Gena. I can understand you not wanting to spend another night in it.'

Elinor Potts had the light of battle in her eyes. 'We'll find out who did this, Gena. Dr Maddison has been talking to everyone here already. And woe betide them for depriving us of the best young doctor we've ever had!' She paused. 'Richard will be very sorry to lose you.' Had Gena been able to look at anything but the floor at this point, she might have seen Matron making a rather searching examination of her face. But the moment passed quickly as she added in more cheerful tones, 'But you'll be back. When this is all cleared up, we'll see you back here. We'll just say goodbye for now.'

'Yes,' said Gena, 'I'll say it here, to you all. I don't think I could cope with a public send-off. I've always cried at bus-stops and train stations.'

Matron smiled. 'Very well, we'll say goodbye now. And thanks, Dr Lamb.'

Gena didn't know what to do now. It was only ten o'clock. She said goodbye to some patients, but it didn't take long; the hospital was not full now. And she was beginning to feel she couldn't cope with any more goodbyes. How could she fill the day in? How to keep her mind off the one goodbye that mattered most?

She would walk. It came to her suddenly. There was one place she had always wanted to walk to, and she had never got there. It was a low hill, several miles distant on the south-western plain behind the hospital. Walking would help her.

She filled a small plastic bottle with water in the kitchen and put it in her shoulder-bag. She stuffed her hat on her head, and set off across the yellow grasslands under a clear blue sky. No worry about hyenas now, in the broad light of the morning. It wasn't their way, she had learned.

She made herself walk quickly. The physical effort would take her mind off her mental pain. And the rocky little hill was further, perhaps, than she'd thought. Four miles, perhaps five? She thought she could get there and be back by two o'clock if she hurried. It gave her something to concentrate on.

Sweat was running in rivulets down Gena's spine as the sun beat down on her back. She stopped for a moment and looked at her watch. Eleven-thirty—crazy time to be out walking. She took a drink from her bottle. The hill was near now, though, perhaps another mile. She must have walked four miles in the hour. The hospital was hidden over a rise in the plain.

One more mile. It would take her half an hour, she thought. The grass was longer here, knee-deep in places, and it slowed her down. She slung her bag over the other shoulder and strode out, her eyes on the approaching hill.

Gena didn't see it. Her eyes were on her goal as she hurried forward through the grass and stepped into nothingness. Only a circling hawk saw the girl try to save herself, too late, from the mouth of the yawning hole. She gave a shrill cry as she fell through space, then lay stunned on hard earth below.

Several seconds passed before her mind could grasp what had come to pass. She was winded, and her first priority was getting her breath. It came in hard gasps as she lay on the dirt floor. Gradually, though, it grew easier. And she knew where she was. She was at the bottom of a well—one of those wells that Richard, eons ago, had told her about.

She sat up slowly, trying to assess the damage. Her ribs were sore, and her left knee and elbow. She didn't think she had hit her head, and her back was all right. Clearly, she had landed on her side.

She tried to straighten her elbow. It hurt, but she could do it. The same with her knee. Gena pressed on her ribs at the side. One of them hurt like hell—probably broken. Well, it could have been worse. And now, with her injuries catalogued, she applied her mind to her situation. Painfully, she drew herself to her feet and surveyed her resting place. There was a smooth earth floor, free of scorpions, she was pleased to see. The sides of the well were also packed smooth. It was well dug. There were no irregularities worthy of the name, no handholds or footholds in the side to climb up on. The depth was more than twice her height, about twelve feet, she estimated. It was six feet across, maybe a few inches more. Too wide for her to wedge herself with feet and arms and climb up that way, as she'd seen in a movie once.

For the first time since she had fallen, Gena felt a tiny thrill of fear. She could be in trouble here. Keep calm, she told herself out loud, and sat down again, leaning against the side this time and looking up.

Very little thought was needed to come to the conclusion that there was no way out. Not without help. A little surge of panic met this sure deduction, but she fought it down. OK, she told herself, you can't get out. You're a long way from home and there's no one out here. There's no point in wearing yourself out shouting. But you're not badly hurt, you have some water, and they're going to miss you and come looking for you.

Right, said a small dissenting voice. They'll look for you. But will they find you? Did you say where you were going?

Gena swore. 'Damn!' she muttered. 'I'm a fool! Why didn't I remember what he said about these things? Why didn't I tell someone where I was going? At least they'd know where to start.'

It dawned on her that it could take them days. They'd find her, she felt sure of that. When they missed her, they'd look till they did, if they had to peer into every dry well in the Central Sudan.

And at that depressing moment, Gena made her second unwelcome discovery. The plastic bottle had shattered in the fall. She had no water at all.

At Udari Central Hospital, lunch was being placed on the sideboard by a Gudwe more silent than normally.

'Where's Gena?' asked Richard, when she didn't appear for lunch.

'Probably gone for a walk,' the Matron guessed wisely, and added quietly, 'She told us she was leaving.'

Richard's eyes flicked up for a moment to meet her steady ones and look away again. 'Did she?' he said. 'I'll be sorry to lose her help, but I think it's her best decision. I won't feel easy till she's a long way away from here.'

'Did you find anything out?' asked Matron. He shook his head.

Presently they spoke of other things. 'I'm taking Pauline with me down to the town now,' Richard told them. 'We've got some home calls to do. We won't be back till dark.'

Elinor Potts registered surprise for a moment, then thought better of it. That's right, my boy, she said to herself. I'm not surprised you can't bear to see her leave. Out loud, she said nothing.

Gena looked at her watch. It was still going. She had been down here two hours. A while to go yet before they would miss her. By three o'clock, she judged, they would wonder. At four, they would worry. When she didn't turn up for the ride to the plane, they'd know that something was wrong.

She changed her position. She was glad she'd had that drink before she fell. It had to be acknowledged that the chances of being found tonight were slim. They would head for her accustomed walks first. This would not be high on their list.

But she would hear them, and that would be encouraging. Across the open plain, in the still night air, you could hear an engine for miles. It would keep her going.

At four o'clock the parking area near the out-patients' clinic was deserted, and so was the residence. Jonathan and Angus were late back from Tempulu. Richard and Pauline were in the town.

Gudwe, working on an engine in the maintenance shed, knew an impulse to run down to where the truck waited, and see Gena one more time. But he didn't. She didn't want it. It would make her cry, perhaps, and he couldn't bear that.

Elinor Potts was in the ward. She also would respect Gena's wishes, and see that the African nurses did the same.

Only Heather Anderson slipped out of the wards and round the back of the outpatients' clinic to stand in the shadows and watch the young doctor's departure. She couldn't help it. The plane had landed; they had heard it overhead. The truck was late. But presently the African driver left the hospital kitchen and traversed the yard to the truck. He glanced in the back to see that all was where he'd left it. He swung himself into the cabin.

No one waited for him in the yard. No one sprang from the residence veranda when he started the engine. No one had told him anything. He put it in gear, and drove away.

And in the shadows by the outpatients' clinic, a girl in a sister's uniform stood, frowning and thinking.

Gena heard the plane come and go. Now, she thought. Now they'll start looking.

At six o'clock, Richard and Pauline returned from the town. Jonathan and Angus had been back an hour, and were already ensconced on the veranda with drinks.

'How did you go?' asked Richard as he mounted the veranda steps.

'Pretty well,' answered Angus. 'The water there's not bad at the moment.'

Richard sat down in a chair. 'Where's Gena?' he asked.

'I don't know,' Angus said. 'We thought she must be with you.'

'Maybe she's in the wards,' said Richard. 'Here's Elinor now.'

'I'll be glad when the cool comes tonight,' confided Matron as she came to stand on the veranda. 'It's been a terrible day. Nothing went right this afternoon.'

She seemed about to enlarge on this theme, when her flow of speech was halted completely by Richard's question. 'Where's Gena?'

She looked at him blankly for a moment, and he raised an eyebrow enquiringly. She stuttered a little, then finally found her voice again.

'Well, she's gone, of course,' she said.

It was Richard's turn to look blank. 'Gone?' he echoed.

Matron Potts sat down abruptly in the chair behind her, as she began to have an idea of what had happened. 'Oh, my goodness!' she exclaimed. 'You didn't know she was going today!'

The silence on the veranda seemed to last for a very long time.

'Today?' he repeated dully.

'Well, yes,' sputtered Matron, for once at a loss. 'She came and said she was going today. I had no idea she hadn't told you. When you said you were going to town—well, I naturally thought you'd already said your goodbyes. You remember, I mentioned her leaving at lunchtime, Richard.'

'Not today,' said Richard softly. 'You didn't say today.'

'Oh, my goodness!' repeated Matron.

Jonathan was less moderate. 'Bloody hell!' he snapped.

Angus cleared his throat. 'You're not to blame her, any of you,' he said firmly. 'You—you don't know how she felt, you see. She spoke to me this morning, about whether she should leave. She was terribly upset about having to leave here. She told me she couldn't bear to say goodbye. That's obviously why she's done as she has.'

'Where has she gone?' Jonathan demanded. 'Khartoum?'

Angus shook his head. 'No, she said she'd go home.'

Richard jerked his head up, but he didn't speak. And presently he appeared to be looking fixedly at a spot on the veranda rail. His face was unreadable. Finally he got up and walked out into the gathering dark.

Dinner that evening was not a very gay affair. Even Heather was silent, though she seemed more restless than ever and chewed abstractedly at her fingernails.

It was dark in the well now; by the luminous dial of her watch, Gena could see it was half-past eight. She wondered whether it was really as cold as it seemed, or whether it was the silence that was chilling her.

The night was as still as death. Had there been a truck out there within about three miles she would have heard it, she thought. What had gone wrong? Why weren't they looking for her?

For the first time since she fell down the hole, she felt the tears pricking at her. She let them come and cried for a little, because she was cold and hungry and hurt, and for the loneliness of it.

At length she wiped them away, however. They would come. They would drive out to the acacias first, and work there south across the plain. She tried to calculate how long it would take them, if they started at five o'clock. Midnight, she thought. They would have to be in the area by then. She would hear them by then.

At nine-thirty, Richard was sitting in the darkness on the steps of the ward block. A few minutes later he rose abruptly and strode into the hospital building with the gait of a man who had made a decision. He came to the room where the radio was and entered it. At nine thirty-five, he had switched on the set.

Across the yard on the veranda of the residence, only Jonathan and Pauline remained in their chairs.

They hadn't often sat together like this. But tonight, something kept them both there.

Jonathan didn't often speak to her, but he did so now.

'Pauline,' he said, 'do you believe she'd go like that?' He peered at her through the dark. He could see her eyes shining.

Her voice when it came shocked him. It was emphatic. 'I don't believe it—not Dr Lamb. She was different. She had principles. She was a fine person.'

Jonathan sat forward. 'Pauline,' he said urgently, 'what the hell has happened?'

'I don't know, Dr Haywood. And I don't like it. Something terrible must have happened to make her go like that. I know it's un-Christian to make accusations without any evidence, but tomorrow morning I'm going to do an un-Christian thing!'

Gena had slept for a while, curled up on the floor of the well on her good side. When she awoke, she looked at her watch and started up eagerly. She listened. It was twelve-thirty; she must hear them now. She held her breath.

There was nothing.

She was filled with a feeling of suffocating panic. Her knees felt weak and she sank to the floor. In a moment, she was sobbing. What if they never came for her? What if they never found her here?

Then she would die.

The very enormity of the thought stilled her. She leant back against the side of the well and let her mind dwell on what she had not allowed into consciousness before.

If they didn't come for her, she would die.

What were the chances of that? The real question was: what could stop them coming for her? Work backwards, she told herself. They wouldn't come if they hadn't missed her. Keep going, keep going. They wouldn't have missed her—if—if no one had seen the truck leave for the plane. Her bags would have gone, so they'd assume she had too.

Gena's mind reeled. Could that have happened? She stared into the darkness, thinking wildly. Gudwe—no, he wouldn't have been there. She'd told him not to come back to see her off. Matron and Heather wouldn't have, either. They would have stayed at their work.

Jonathan and Angus they could have arrived back late. They often did. But Pauline and Richard. They should have been waiting for her. Matron would have told them at lunchtime.

Gena went cold. What if she hadn't, and they had gone off somewhere? What if they'd been called away at four o'clock? What if Richard had decided he didn't want to say goodbye? What if no one had been there? She already knew the answer; that was where she had started. She would die.

She lay on her back and looked up. Above her was a small circle of black velvet sky studded with shining stars. Hot tears ran over the sides of her face, down her neck and into her ears. It was the stars that made her cry—they were so beautiful.

How many more times would she see them? The top of the well for Gena was as far away as those stars.

'Richard!' she cried. 'Oh, God, make him come!'

At three o'clock she woke again. She was frozen. Soon she realised what had woken her. It came again, the strange disturbing cry she had heard in the Nuba hills. There were hyenas out here too.

How she longed for Richard's arms now, holding her like a child. It came closer, and she shivered with fear. Could hyenas jump down wells and get out again?

No, surely not. It was twelve feet deep. Maybe they could jump six, or even eight, but not twelve. It was the only reason she could think of to be glad of being at the bottom of a twelve-foot hole.

At eleven o'clock the next day, Richard left the residence. He walked towards the truck which was waiting in the yard. Gudwe had the engine going. Richard landed in the passenger's seat in one graceful movement, and in another moment they had moved off through the hospital gates towards the airstrip.

An hour later, Pauline Hickey found Heather alone in the hospital dispensary. She entered after her, and resolutely locked the door.

It was hot again. Gena knew it was noon without having to look at her watch. The sun was beating down her well. She sat huddled over with her head on her knees. She was thirsty. She had spent the

cool hours of the morning thinking of Richard,
trying to relive every pleasant moment he had given
her. It was all she would ever have of him.

She remembered every time his grey eyes had met
hers and her heart had turned over. Stupid
expression, thought the doctor in her—anatomically
impossible for a heart to turn over! She remembered
every kind, friendly word he had said to her, every
smile of approval. She felt again the touch of his
hand on her arm in Khartoum, when she had let
herself believe that there was a promise of happiness
in it. And their one kiss, which had ignited emotions
in her she hadn't known she could feel.

She could see his face, and lingered lovingly over
the vision—the curling dark hair, the broad forehead, the straight nose and strong chin, the seductive
curve of his mouth, and most of all those clear grey
eyes.

She tried to believe in telepathy and to send him
a message. Heather believed in it, quite seriously. If
only she were right! Her tongue felt dry. She looked
at the skin on the back of her hand. Still plenty of
moisture in it. She wouldn't die today—or even
tomorrow, she thought. The day after that her
kidneys would start to fail. Even then it would take
some time for the coma to steal up on her and the
convulsions to start. Death was going to be very
slow and very unpleasant.

In the afternoon she thought of her parents. They
would never know what had happened to her—not
until someone stumbled on her remains.

'Oh, Mum,' she sobbed aloud, 'I'm sorry!'

What would Peter say? Poor old Peter. Perhaps he'd say, I told her so. No, of course he'd be sorry. But it didn't matter any more. Peter was such a long way in the past.

As the sun receded again and there was a cool spot to sit in, she found herself weaving fantasies of rescue over and over. She could hear the truck, closer and closer, the men's voices, Richard's calling to her, then his arms around her, magically. Sometimes there would be a helicopter to lift her out of the well; other times a rope ladder appeared over the side. But always Richard's face, his comforting words, his strong hands, his——

Gena jerked herself upright and sat stock-still on the floor of the well. Her heart pounded in her ears, the blood rushing to her head. She held her breath and stared straight ahead, her eyes large and round. Gradually the thudding of her heart subsided and she could hear it again. She could hear it!

Or was it a hallucination, a part of the fantasies she'd been weaving?

She scrambled to her feet and stood still, her ear inclined to the mouth of the well. She could hear it—the engine of a truck.

She leant against the side of the well, and covered her face and prayed.

'Oh, please! Oh, please, God!' And even as she prayed for it, the sound came louder and nearer.

*　*　*

The man in the Land Rover drove it over the grassy, rutted plain as though he had several more at home to replace it. It hit the hillocks and holes and bounced and swayed, but he drove on in disregard. Another man, an African, sat on the passenger's window-sill, his body hanging perilously outside the truck, looking ahead.

Gena shouted. Over and over, till her throat hurt and she was breathless, she shouted for help. This was her chance for life. They might drive past.

She heard the engine pause for a moment, and shouted even more desperately. 'Oh, God, stop! Don't go away!'

The engine noise ceased altogether. Had she imagined it? Or, joyful thought, were they listening for her? She shouted till her voice cracked. The engine started again. And now time stretched out to an eternity, as Gena endeavoured to shape the events of the future by sheer effort of will. Her whole existence hummed and throbbed with the engine of a truck, grew into life as it advanced, shrank into nothingness as it receded.

And then it seemed to advance again. It seemed to come directly towards her, louder and louder till it was right above her, and she heard the engine switch off, and running feet and the most blessed sound she'd ever heard, her shouted name.

'Gena!' The voice she'd imagined. Was she imagining this?

'Richard!' A sobbing reply.

She heard their voices, and saw movements at the top of the well, and in another moment the end of a rope had dropped to the floor beside her and a man had swung himself down it with easy grace and was holding her as though he was afraid she would run away.

Gena cried.

'My poor darling,' said the man, stroking her hair and pressing her face to his chest. 'My poor little girl!'

'R—Richard!' she sobbed.

'Ssh!' he said gently. 'It's all right now. Nothing can hurt you. Nothing will ever hurt you again.'

'Try that!' came a voice from the top. It was a makeshift ladder, of rope.

'Can you cling to me?' Richard asked, and Gena nodded. 'Put your arms round my neck and your legs round my waist.' He lifted her like a child.

And in a few moments they had reached the top, and the world stretched out before her, a limitless world of wide brown plains as far as she could see, meeting a vast blue sky.

He sat her down in the back of the truck and sat on the tray beside her, his arms still round her. She still cried. Gudwe poured out some water, and Richard took it and put it to her lips.

'Were you hurt in the fall?' he asked, and she shook her head and continued to drink between sobs.

She leant back, finished, and found her tongue. 'I'd like you to know,' she said, 'that I haven't spent the *whole* time crying.' Richard's face slowly relaxed. And even more slowly, his mouth curved into a smile that Gena felt she would have given the whole world and every moment of the rest of her life to see. And finally, he even laughed, and so did the others, and so did she.

And Richard hugged her again, and Gudwe and Angus, and then she found herself laughing and crying together.

CHAPTER THIRTEEN

GENA rested against the pillows and refused absolutely the last mouthful that Richard was trying to get her to eat.

'I was only there a day,' she protested. 'I'm not dying of starvation!'

She was washed and dressed in a clean nightie now, and her bruised knee and elbow had been inspected and pronounced to be in one piece. Her rib was broken, but her lung was undamaged.

Richard was sitting on her bed. He was being terribly kind.

'I think I know what happened,' said Gena. 'Nobody saw the truck go.' She looked at Richard and he nodded.

'Elinor tells me you didn't want a send-off party. Jonathan and Angus were still at Tempulu, and Pauline and I were in Udari. I didn't know you were going.'

'Matron didn't tell you?'

'She assumed I knew.'

Gena gave a short mirthless laugh and closed her eyes. 'Oh, lord, what a brilliant mess I made of all that!'

'What a brilliant mess *I* made of it, Gena. I didn't question it, you see. I—I could well believe you might leave without saying goodbye after our—disagreement—the night before.'

'I understand. Only—I wouldn't have, Richard, even so. I owe you too much. The things you've taught me here. . .your kindness——'

'Don't!' he said, his voice strained. 'I don't deserve it. None of this would have happened if I hadn't tried to manipulate you.'

Gena couldn't quite see that he'd done that, but it didn't matter now. 'What I want to know, then, is how did you work out I hadn't gone?'

Richard paused a moment. 'I didn't work it out— I found it out,' he said. 'I radioed for the plane to come back next day and take me to Khartoum. When he got here, I found there'd been no passengers the afternoon before.'

Gena looked at him, her eyes wide. 'Then it was sheer luck,' she breathed. 'If you hadn't had a reason to go to Khartoum next day. . .'

He raised an eyebrow at her. 'Well, not entirely luck. After all, you were the reason that I had to go there.'

'What do you mean?' she asked.

'The plane to Nairobi left at four-thirty that afternoon. It was my intention to be at the airport in Khartoum before you got on it.'

Gena's heart had suddenly quickened its pace. Her mouth felt unaccountably dry again. She told herself she was stupid for the wild hope that arose within her. Naturally he wouldn't have wanted her to leave like that. He must have been glad she'd decided to go, but he was a decent man. He wouldn't have wanted it to end with such bitterness.

'That was nice of you,' she said in a small voice, and tried not to feel the pain as his grey eyes fastened on hers.

Slowly he shook his head. 'No,' he said hoarsely, 'not nice—desperate.'

Gena frowned. 'What do you mean?'

He made an impatient movement. 'I've made a mess of things from beginning to end. I alienated you in the beginning, because I didn't think you were suitable for Africa. You're so lovely, Gena.' His voice sounded pained.

She blushed. 'I knew you didn't like me,' she said.

'That wasn't it. You look—so delicate. And, if I were to tell the truth, I would have to say that there was an element of self-preservation in my disapproval of you too.' He looked at her again. 'I think I unconsciously knew from the start that you could be trouble for me. I didn't want to—become involved with someone who would inevitably leave again, who probably would never fit in.

'And then,' he continued, 'by the time I realised that you did fit in, and that you were superb here, and that, even more importantly, I felt what I did about you, there was Jonathan.'

'I don't understand. What did you——?'

'It made me angry. That's irrational, I know, but it made me angry that you cared for him.'

'But I didn't!' cried Gena.

'I know,' he said softly, his voice full of pain. 'At

least, I knew at Khartoum when you told me. I should have taken my chance then, shouldn't I? But I left it too late.'

Gena stared at him, trying to understand. 'I don't know what you mean. Your chance for what? Yesterday you told me—you wanted me to leave.' Her heart was thumping again.

'Yes, I did—and I don't expect you to forgive me for that. But I would like you to understand. I could see you wouldn't go to protect yourself, so I had to find another way to get you to safety. I thought you might leave if I made you feel I wanted you to go.'

The world seemed to stand balanced on a knife's edge for Gena. What was he saying? 'Do you mean—that kiss? It wasn't a mistake?' She raised her eyes to him.

'Oh, Gena!' His voice was choked. 'You'll just have to forgive me. It was no more a mistake than this one.'

And in the kiss he gave her now, and the arms that clutched her to him, Gena at last knew certainty. When finally he freed her lips, she found herself trembling and weak.

'Forgive me,' he was murmuring into her hair. 'I was so afraid. I love you so much.'

'Oh, Richard,' she whispered, the tears welling up in her eyes, 'I love you too,' and there was no conversation at all for a while.

'I'd never intended to let you go further away than Khartoum,' he said at last. 'When I heard you were going home, I couldn't bear it.'

'Oh, Richard, I'm so glad!' She looked up at him. 'I wish you'd just told me. I would have gone to Khartoum and waited.'

'I know that now. I wish I had too.'

'I suppose I must go still.'

He shook his head and smiled. 'No. Pauline has solved that mystery for us. There's no need for you to leave now.'

Gena looked at him intently. 'How?' she asked.

'She knew you better than I did. She didn't believe you would leave that way unless something extraordinary had happened. She never believed you'd made that mistake with the drug. And she suspected that Heather had something to do with it. She had no evidence at all, but she couldn't help thinking that Heather had something to do with your hasty departure as well.'

'Heather!' Gena sat bolt upright. She groped for meaning in her mind. Pauline. Heather. Their faces swam before her—Pauline's brooding, with burning eyes, a face full of passion; Heather's ordinary in comparison, without much feeling at all. 'But surely it was Pauline. . .' Her brain span.

Richard looked at her, comprehending. 'Did you suspect Pauline of doing those things?' Dumbly she nodded. He shook his head. 'No, Gena. Pauline will never be your enemy. She'll be your ally for life, whether you want it or not. I don't think it would be too much to say that she's become as devoted to you as she is to me and Elinor. I might have had a lot more trouble finding you if Pauline hadn't done what she considers a rather un-Christian thing. . .' He smiled gently. 'She confronted Heather and forced her to tell her everything. I'm not sure how she did it, except that Heather has always had some strange ideas. She's rather afraid of Pauline, in the same way that some of the Africans are.'

'But Richard, was it Heather?'

'I'm afraid it was, my love—the blood tubes, the overdose, the scorpion. And she knew you didn't leave for the airport in the truck. She watched you, you see. Which was lucky, because it meant she knew which way you'd gone. And Pauline found that out for us.'

'But I don't understand why. . .' And yet, as she spoke, there darted through her mind a series of images, the pieces of another jigsaw. Heather explaining how Richard liked things done. Heather anxious and troubled at the end of their patrol. A secretly triumphant Heather after the drug overdose. And her face as Gena and Richard left for Khartoum—taut, pale, strained, a little desperate.

And Gena found herself able to imagine another Heather—the junior nurse who had loved a doctor so much that she had followed him to Africa, and who believed, perhaps, that time and African magic would make him love her too.

'Oh, God,' she groaned, 'what a fool I've been!' And a vision of Pauline arose too—the vision of the dream—a devoted, protective Pauline, a woman whom she had not been able to fear because there had been nothing to fear from her.

'No more than I,' said Richard softly. 'When Heather came out here, I thought I'd inspired her with a desire to work in Africa. I didn't realise—that she cared for me and not the work till Pauline told me today. That's why she wanted you away from here, you see. She knew what was happening between us. It was a disaster for her.'

'Poor Heather!' said Gena softly.

Richard smiled gently. 'How like you! Still, I don't think she really wanted to hurt anyone, Gena. I think she lives in a fantasy world at times. She convinced herself that the child wouldn't die from the drug and that the scorpion wouldn't bite you. But perhaps she couldn't quite convince herself that keeping quiet about your disappearance was all right. Pauline feels she was relieved to be forced to tell about it.'

Gena nodded. 'I understand. She wanted you so much. And the gods had given her a way. . . What will happen to her now?'

'She's going back to London. I feel she needs some treatment.'

'You mean—a psychiatrist?'

'Yes. She really is——' he sought the correct words '—not in touch with reality.'

Gena bit her lip. 'I really have maligned Pauline horridly, haven't I?'

She looked up at him and saw his face fill with humour. 'Don't worry, love. Pauline's very big on Christian forgiveness.' And he added, 'I don't think psychiatry is your strong point, my darling.'

Gena grinned somewhat ruefully. 'I'm coming to that conclusion myself,' she said.

Richard leaned back on her pillow and took her in his arms again. He looked down at her with the grey eyes that could do such unanatomical things to her heart.

'I can see I've got a lot of things to teach you,' he said. 'It will take me a lifetime, I'm afraid.'

Discover the thrill of 4 Exciting Medical Romances – FREE

BOOKS FOR YOU

In the exciting world of modern medicine, the emotions of true love have an added drama. Now you can experience four of these unforgettable romantic tales of passion and heartbreak FREE – and look forward to a regular supply of Mills & Boon Medical Romances delivered direct to your door!

🐾 🐾 🐾

Turn the page for details of 2 extra free gifts, and how to apply.

An Irresistible Offer from Mills & Boon

Here's an offer from Mills & Boon to become a regular reader of Medical Romances. To welcome you, we'd like you to have four books, a cuddly teddy and a special MYSTERY GIFT, all absolutely free and without obligation.

Then, every two months you could look forward to receiving 6 more **brand new** Medical Romances for £1.35 each, delivered direct to your door, post and packing free. Plus our newsletter featuring author news, competitions, special offers, and lots more.

This invitation comes with no strings attached. You can cancel or suspend your subscription at any time, and still keep your free books and gifts.

Its so easy. Send no money now. Simply fill in the coupon below and post it at once to -

**Mills & Boon Reader Service, FREEPOST,
PO Box 236, Croydon, Surrey CR9 9EL**

NO STAMP REQUIRED

- - - >%- - - - - - - - - - - - - - - - - -

YES! Please rush me my 4 Free Medical Romances and 2 Free Gifts! Please also reserve me a Reader Service Subscription. If I decide to subscribe, I can look forward to receiving 6 brand new Medical Romances every two months for just £8.10, delivered direct to my door. Post and packing is free, and there's a free Mills & Boon Newsletter. If I choose not to subscribe I shall write to you within 10 days - I can keep the books and gifts whatever I decide. I can cancel or suspend my subscription at any time. I am over 18.

Name (Mr/Mrs/Ms) _____ EP90D

Address _____

_____

_____ Postcode _____

Signature _____